A Reluctant Traitor

By
John Pilkington

Table of Contents

ONE

TWO

THREE

FOUR

FIVE

SIX

SEVEN

EIGHT

NINE

TEN

ELEVEN

TWELVE

THIRTEEN

FOURTEEN

FIFTEEN

ONE

On a bitterly cold morning, after the castle of Falaise had fallen to King Henri IV's army of French and English troops and assorted mercenaries, Captain Will Revill found himself challenged to a duel.

At first, since all about him was now at peace, he thought it must be a mistake. The siege of Falaise had been short, and less troublesome than he and his crew had feared. Though his old sergeant Tom Bright, now corporal of gunnery, had grumbled that he would have preferred to spend Christmas in comfort, with a mug of something warm, instead of firing cannonballs at castle walls. But that was over a week ago, and since the town was taken the English contingent had been at rest, awaiting orders from their commander Lord Willoughby. The word was that the King's force would move south, but Willoughby himself, though still a young man, was exhausted and ready to take his troops home: a prospect relished by all. Already, it was said, more Englishmen had died of cold, disease and bad food than had perished in battle.

Revill, clad in a woollen coat, surveyed the frozen fields and winter-bare trees on the edge of the encampment. Normandy was a beautiful land, he had decided, even if scarred by civil war. But he was thinking of home, and

1

naturally of his lover Jenna, when a young French *caporal* appeared before him, made a swift bow and held out a paper.

'What's this – I mean, *qu'est-ce que c'est*?' Revill asked, looking him up and down. He was not an infantryman, but a *brigadier* of horse. When the man merely pointed, he opened the letter and read - only to lower it in disbelief.

'*Un duel*?' He frowned. 'What in God's name…?'

'Is a matter of honour, monsieur', the young Frenchman said, in heavily-accented English. 'Capitaine Dufort, he has no quarrel with yourself, but with your *caporal*. Since it is below his dignity to challenge a common soldier to combat, you as his *commandant* must act on his behalf. It is, as you say, your *responsibilité*.'

'But that's absurd,' Revill retorted. 'I have no desire to fight this… Captain Dufort. We're on the same side, are we not? While I'm sure the enemy would love to see an Englishman and a Frenchman at each other's throats, doubtless Lord Willoughby and your Marshal Biron would think differently, would they not?'

'If you read the entire letter, monsieur, you will see it is a personal matter,' came the stiff reply. 'To be conducted in private. The Capitaine suggests *le bois* – the wood – as the place.'

'Wait… one minute.' Only now, Revill realised, had the words sunk in: the mention of his *caporal*. His suspicions soaring, he was about to ask the other what quarrel his commander could possibly have with Tom Bright. But instead he bade the man stay, before turning smartly and walking over to one of the battered and threadbare tents, where his men were quartered. Lifting the flap, he poked his head inside.

'Corporal Bright!' He snapped. 'Get yourself out here – now.'

Bright, sitting muffled in a fur-trimmed cape he had stolen from somewhere, got to his feet. 'News, Captain?' He enquired hopefully. 'Are we to march, or–'

'Outside, I said,' Revill ordered.

He glanced at the rest of the crew, gathered around a brazier of hot coals. The oldest, Dan Newcome, a veteran of the Scots campaign of thirty years back, threw him a wary look: it did not sound like good news to him. The younger men, however – the Kentish brothers Martin and Edward Kitto, and the boy, Lambert Bowen – brightened at once. For a second, Revill felt almost ashamed: they were good men, brave and loyal, and had done well in the short months he had been their gun-master. But having tasted battle now – the numbing brutality of it, let alone the grim conditions of the camp - their enthusiasm for soldiering had faded considerably. Like Tom Bright, they were eager to go home.

Dropping the flap, he stepped from the tent and waited for his one-time sergeant to emerge. Whereupon, before he could open his mouth, Revill waved the letter at him.

'What do you know about a certain captain of horse named Dufort?' He demanded - and at once, Bright's face fell.

'Well, in truth I know very little,' he replied, a sheepish look forming.

'And yet?' Revill prodded.

'It's, well… I may have made acquaintance, you could say, of a certain lady. One who is known to the officer you mention, and-'

'By the Christ, Tom.' His captain let out a sigh of exasperation. 'Don't tell me you foined his mistress, you-'

'No, I never!' Bright broke in. 'I only spoke with her… polite conversation. She was about to go out riding, and I was talking with the forage master… it was nothing, I swear.'

'You dolt!' Revill exploded. 'She's an officer's lady, and you've insulted him!'

'But I didn't know that,' his corporal protested. 'I only knew her name – Madelon. She was friendly enough. She never said aught about being spoken for, or such…' he trailed off, eyeing the paper in Revill's fist. 'Has there been a complaint?'

'Oh, no complaint,' Revill answered, his voice heavy with sarcasm. 'He only holds me responsible, you being just a common soldier, and demands satisfaction. In short, I must meet him at first light tomorrow, sword at the ready, and fight a duel.'

4

'Sweet Jesus.' Bright gulped, lowering his gaze. 'I'm truly sorry, Captain.'

'Sorry?' Revill echoed. 'You will be, if I perish by Dufort's sword – or maybe even sorrier if I don't. For killing one of his officers, King Henri would have me hanged.'

'Could I not go and ask forgiveness?' Bright suggested, looking forlorn. 'Say it was a misunderstanding, or I mistook Madelon for someone else, or-'

'Too late, I'd say. And he wouldn't even speak with you.'

Both of them fell silent after that. In spite of himself, Revill felt his anger ebbing away. He and his old stalwart had shared so much: their time fighting for the Queen in the Low Countries, then the past year in which they had tried to live quietly back in England, only for Revill to be forced into a desperate mission to assassinate the eccentric knight Sir Abel Stanbury. At times, he still felt lucky that, despite the old man's sad death, he had avoided being to blame. And now, here he was in France in the depths of winter, still under the yoke of the ruthless Vice-Chamberlain Sir Thomas Heneage, charged with spying on his fellow officers. In one way, he drew a grim satisfaction from the fact that he had been too busy marching about and fighting to do any such thing. Having lugged their two culverins through wind and rain from Dieppe down to Alençon, his gun crew had arrived too late for the battle. The northward march here, over wooded hills, had been just as hard. The siege of Falaise had been the crew's first real engagement.

'Could we not put our heads together, Captain, and do something to put the Frenchman off? Delay him, say - or slip something in his brandy?'

Bright's question broke Revill's thoughts. He was about to utter some withering retort - but instead, laughter threatened to break forth. Suppressing it, he forced a frown.

'Don't talk nonsense. Even if that were possible, it would look highly suspicious. My only course is to reply to Dufort's letter, make apology for your insolence and promise to discipline you.'

'A flogging, you mean?' The little corporal blanched. 'That seems a mite harsh, Captain.'

'The promise could avoid swordplay, and buy us time,' Revill told him. 'The order to march should come soon, in any case. In all the activity, everyone would be too busy to think about your punishment.'

Bright breathed a sigh of relief; then his face clouded again. 'What if he won't have your apology? What if he's a haughty bastard, who wants to prove his prowess? There's plenty of that sort in the French-'

'That's enough.' Revill frowned again. 'For now, why don't you go and order the crew to do gunnery practice? It's better than sitting idle in the tent, is it not?'

His corporal blinked, opened his mouth, then closed it again. Revill watched him trudge off with head bowed.

With his thoughts returning to the challenge from a French officer he had never even met, he walked back to the bearer of the dispiriting message.

***

In the afternoon the two culverins, nicknamed Fiery Moll and Spiky Bess, were drawn up alongside each other, their muzzles facing across an open meadow towards the wood. It was the first time either of the eighteen pounders had been fired since they had blown apart the Falaise castle turret, destroying with it a lone musketeer of the Catholic League who had stationed himself bravely atop it and caused many casualties. Young Lambert Bowen – 'Lam' to his fellows - had been almost tearful at what they had done to the courageous marksman. But as the other gunners reminded him, this was battle, and he should count himself lucky he had come through it unscathed. Eager to prove himself now, he was busy cleaning out Fiery Moll's barrel with the sponge-pole. Tom Bright, in a poor temper for reasons the other men could not fathom, shouted at him to hurry up. Dan Newcome, standing with the ramrod at his side, spat on the ground and muttered an oath.

'He does his best,' he growled. 'What's eating at you?'

'None of your affair,' came the retort. 'Look to the loading.'

Martin Kitto came up, carrying a cartouche of powder wrapped in old linen. A man from the Kentish Weald, he was eager to return to the family farm. The only reason he was here was because his young brother had been imprisoned in Newgate, and given a hard choice by the magistrate: a branding and a flogging, or join the army levies for France. Eyeing Tom Bright, he jerked his head towards the culverin.

'How much more powder and shot do you want to waste firing at trees, cannoneer?' He asked. 'Have you got some grudge against poplars?'

'Mayhap he's on commission from the High Marshal,' Newcome muttered. 'A penny a shot, to prove our gunners are better than the French.'

'Waste, you say?' Bright turned on Kitto. 'I'll decide what's wasted and what isn't, as I'll be reporting on your speed and your readiness. You and your jailbird brother.'

The older Kitto stiffened, but he and Newcome exchanged looks, knowing that the corporal meant no real harm; like their captain, he would risk his life for any one of his artillerymen. When Lam Bowen, who had now dried out Fiery Moll's barrel, called that he was done, the two gunners moved to the muzzle to reload. As they shoved the powder bag and wads of oakum down and rammed them home, Edward Kitto arrived to join Bowen: two teenage boys sharing their first experience of warfare, who had quickly become friends.

'Shall we make Spiky Bess ready too?' Edward asked.

'What, when there's barely enough powder left for one shot?' Bright grunted. 'Use your head. Clean her barrel out well, and stuff some oiled rags down. Likely we'll be moving off soon... at least, I hope to God we are,' he added, the last words under his breath. But the two boys had turned sharply, for their captain was approaching.

'That'll be enough for today,' Revill said curtly, as he came up. 'Wheel the guns round. I've asked for horses, to lug them back to the camp.'

'Fiery Moll's just been loaded,' Bright objected. 'I can't unload her.'

'Is the ball already placed?'

Bright glanced at the gunners, who had paused. 'No, only powder and wadding.'

'Then why not shove these down before you fire it off?' He held up a bag, and opened it to show it was full of dried peas. 'But turn her round first, aim at the French camp.'

Bright hesitated, then a wry look appeared. 'It'd scare the life out of them – but if that's what you want?' When Revill said nothing, he called Edward Kitto and Bowen over. Between them, they swivelled the heavy culverin round so that its muzzle faced a distant mass of tents, from where the King's standard could just be seen. Bright pushed a spike through the touchhole to pierce the cartouche, unstopped his flask and poured touching-powder down. Then he walked round to the muzzle, poured the dried peas in, took the ramrod and shoved them home.

Martin Kitto had come round with the linstock already lit, and stood ready.

'Are you sure about this?' He enquired.

9

'That's what the captain wants,' Bright replied, with a sidelong glance at Revill.

With a shrug, the older Kitto stepped back and set the burning match to the hole. There was a splutter as the touching-powder ignited, then a roar and a gush of flame from the culverin's mouth as the charge was fired. The crew stood round, grins appearing as cries of alarm drifted across from the direction of the French camp.

'That'll shake 'em up,' Dan Newcome observed.

'All right - clean her out, and make ready to move off,' Bright said, to no-one in particular. 'Our master has bespoken horses.' As the men fell to their tasks, he took a step towards Revill. 'I get the notion that action wasn't entirely a jest on your part,' he said quietly. 'In truth, it smacked of a grudge.'

Revill eyed him, then gave a curt nod.

'So, your apology wasn't accepted by Monsieur Dufort.'

'No – and there's no need for you to look crestfallen,' his captain retorted. 'You're saved a flogging. While I must meet my challenger tomorrow, as arranged.'

'Did you speak with him?' Bright ventured. 'I mean, what sort of man is-'

'If you must know, he fully merits your description from this morning,' Revill broke in. 'To wit, a haughty bastard who's taken offence and must prove his worth – not least to his fellow officers. He's not the sort who'd stand being mocked.'

The corporal let out a sigh, his gaze drifting towards the crew, who were packing their tools and bags of wadding into wooden chests. Edward Kitto and Lam Bowen had fallen to their usual rough play, pummelling each other as they worked.

'Will there be witnesses?' He enquired. 'I mean, you'll want someone with you. Could I be him, or...?' He broke off, as Revill threw him a scathing look.

'You won't be welcome – Corporal,' he retorted. 'If Dufort knew who you were, he'd likely fight even harder. Then when he'd downed me, he'd down you too on principle.'

'But, what about the men?' Distressed now, Bright gestured towards the gunners. 'Can't I tell them? I mean, don't they have a right...' he stopped himself, shaking his head. 'You're their captain – you know they'd follow you to Hades and back. Who else will command, if you... I mean, if...'

Once again he broke off, his eyes on the ground. For his part, Revill had no words of comfort; to his shame, he realised, since his return empty-handed from his brief visit to Capitaine Dufort earlier that afternoon, he had thought little about the consequences of his crew being left without a commander. He stood in silence, then turned as the others did at the sound of hooves: the horse-teams were arriving, to haul Fiery Moll and Spike Bess back to the encampment.

11

With a heavy heart, he stepped forward to oversee the harnessing of the guns, trying to thrust aside thoughts of his appointment for the morrow. Whether he would be alive after that, to relish the prospect of a march to the Channel coast and eventual return to England, he had no notion.

On a sudden his thoughts turned to Jenna: her voice, uttering familiar words of mingled reproach and affection:

'For pity's sake, Will, what in heaven's name am I to do with you?'

TWO

Dawn came, with a mist rolling up from the River Ante. The camp was barely astir yet, with no cooking-fires even lit. From the picket-lines, horses could be heard snorting and stamping in the cold. When Revill emerged from his tent into the dim light, clad in thick breeches, doublet and a jerkin of leather, he found Tom Bright standing nearby, swinging his arms and beating his chest to warm himself.

'I told you already, you can't come with me,' he said.

'I know,' Bright replied. 'I thought I might bring up the rear, so to speak.'

Revill's brow puckered. 'You haven't breathed a word of this to the others, I hope?'

'No - but it'd take at least two of us to carry your body back, wouldn't it,' the corporal said bitterly. 'If it comes to that, I mean.'

They eyed each other. Finally Revill shook his head, touched his old companion on the arm and looked towards the distant treeline. To think that their years of campaigning together might end in this foolish manner – over a pompous officer's objection to an English soldier flirting with his mistress – made his spirits sink. Gripping the hilt of his freshly-sharpened rapier, he walked quickly away.

13

Bright watched him go, and sighed heavily.

For his captain, it was but a few minutes' walk into the wood and onwards to the clearing he had been told about, by the same young *brigadier* who had delivered yesterday's challenge to single combat. He, along with a French officer, had stood beside the somewhat portly figure of Dufort, when Revill arrived to offer his explanation and apology for the slight the man had suffered. But it was to no avail: Dufort himself had said not a single word, merely eyed Revill with one hand resting on the hilt of his sword. The *capitaine* was looking forward to their meeting on the morrow, the young soldier said. Another officer would be on hand, as his second, along with a surgeon. Having spoken, he had made a brief bow and returned Revill's letter to him.

But now, when he saw the clearing opening ahead of him, Revill slowed his pace: not only were Dufort, another officer and a man who must be the surgeon already waiting, but several others too. As he drew near, he saw to his surprise that they were not Frenchmen, but mercenaries in plainer garb, probably Germans. Only one of them was an officer, he surmised – what function, he wondered, did the others serve?

The question would soon be answered, however. At sight of him the men turned swiftly, and the French officer who was not Dufort strode forward to greet him.

14

'*Bonjour, monsieur*,' he said pleasantly, before changing to rudimentary English. 'I am, I will say, most surprised that you have come alone. How is that?'

'I prefer it this way,' Revill told him, his gaze shifting to the group of men beyond. 'Captain Dufort, however, appears to have brought a small crowd with him. Were you expecting difficulties?'

'No, no.' The other shook his head. 'We… it was thought wise to have witnesses who are not of the King's own countrymen. Captain Werner and his men will observe, but play no part. Later, they will serve as bearers, or…'

He trailed off with a shrug, but Revill believed he understood: the French military leader, Marshal Biron, was unaware of the duel – as, he was sure, was King Henri, who would likely have stopped it. So: should he lose his life, he wondered, did these men propose to bury his corpse here in the wood? In which case, what might his commander Lord Willoughby do?

He met the officer's eye. 'Then, might I ask for your promise that, should I fail – whether I am dead, or merely too badly hurt to continue – you will see that I am conveyed back to my tent, where my own men will attend me?'

'But of course, monsieur,' came the prompt reply. 'It would be an honour.'

He waited, until Revill gave a brief nod and walked forward. When he drew near to the French party he halted, whereupon the surgeon, a grey-haired man with a world-weary air, took a pace forward.

'Are you in good health, *Capitaine*?' He enquired. 'Able and willing to engage?'

Revill replied in the affirmative, then looked at Dufort, who refused to meet his eye. His glance falling on the officer of mercenaries, whom he now knew as Captain Werner, he saw the man eyeing him with interest. Dismissing him, he faced Dufort's fellow officer, who enquired if he was ready.

With a nod, Revill drew his sword and made his salute to his challenger, who did the same. And almost at once, it was time. As the other men fell back, forming a rough circle in the glade, the duellists faced each other. Though outwardly calm, Revill felt tense: this was a fight he had never sought, and did not relish in the slightest. His opponent, however, his breath clouding in the cold, wore a look of contempt – but beneath it, Revill sensed unease. For a moment he wondered whether this was some kind of face-saving exercise on Dufort's part... had he even been chivvied into it by his fellows?

Yet there was no time to speculate. He fell into a fencer's crouch, feeling his pulse quicken. Dufort followed suit, his well-padded frame resting heavily on his short legs. The man was in poor shape, Revill thought briefly – and as a consequence, any fears he might have for his own life began to fade. More likely, perhaps, he would need to face the consequences of winning the engagement – what might follow then?

He forced the other man to meet his gaze, showing his resolve while waiting for him to make his move. He believed he could parry well enough… whereupon something caught his eye that made him start.

No wonder Dufort looked so well-padded and so stiff, he realised: between the buttons of his doublet, stretched across his chest, Revill saw a glint of metal. Under his clothing, the man was wearing a breast-plate of steel.

'Stop!' He exclaimed. 'You are armoured, sir – this won't do.'

His answer was an oath he did not understand, whereupon Dufort lunged with surprising speed, catching Revill off guard. Dipping aside quickly, he barely managed to meet the other's rapier, the clash of steel upon steel ringing in the crisp air. Then their sword-hilts engaged and they were face to face, breathing hard as they vied for mastery.

'I demand that you cease, Captain,' Revill breathed. 'You wear a cuirass and I have none, which is ignoble-'

But he broke off as the other man, using his ample body-weight, forced him to take a backward step. Dufort fell back too, lifting his sword for another stroke. With rising anger, Revill levelled his own rapier, at the same time calling to the man's supporters.

'Gentlemen, you should call a halt!' He shouted, keeping his eyes on his opponent. 'This man carries the advantage of armour - he is without honour!'

There was a murmur of voices, a rapid exchange of French which Revill failed to catch. From the corner of his eye, he saw the surgeon addressing Dufort's second, while Werner and his men stood apart in silence. Thoughts raced through his brain: was this a trap of some sort? And were the mercenaries there to step in, should he be the victor? Bending low, his gaze fixed on his opponent's sword-arm, he tried to judge what stroke the man would make next - until there came a shout that changed everything.

'*Arrêtez! Le roi l'inderdit… attendez*!'

Revill turned sharply, as did Dufort and the others, as a figure in plain livery rode out of the trees on a fine Spanish horse with a white blaze on its forehead. At his approach, both duellists and spectators reacted, while Revill lowered his sword. Dufort, after muttering something under his breath, lowered his also, a sickly look on his fleshy features. Watched by everyone, the newcomer, who clearly carried some authority, reined in and looked down at them. Dufort, with a glare at his opponent, moved away to stand beside his fellow officer. But Revill breathed a deep sigh of relief. He had understood the envoy's words: the duel must cease, because the King had forbidden it.

He sheathed his sword and waited. For a while, there followed a heated exchange among the French party. But after the messenger had dismounted and spoken further, things grew calmer. Though only the surgeon, Revill thought, looked relieved: Dufort and his friend were displeased. Once again, he allowed his gaze to drift towards the mercenaries, who looked on warily. But the outcome, he knew, was plain enough: either his own life, or that of his challenger, had been saved in timely fashion by order of the King. From savouring the development, he was starting to think about the consequences for himself should the High Marshal hear about it, when a voice was raised. Looking round, he saw that the envoy, now revealed to be a youthful, slender man with dark curly hair, was walking towards him.

'Captain Revill?' He spoke in an unmistakeable London accent. 'I'm Guy Baildon. I carry word from the muster-master: Willoughby will march for Caen today.'

In rising relief, Revill could only stare at him.

'Come, be not amazed,' the other added. 'Do I sound like a Frenchman? I'm not the only one in our army who knows the language – you speak a little yourself, from what I hear.'

'Well, but…' Still taking in the situation, Revill raised his brows. 'You said the King had forbidden this… this business, so I thought-'

'Oh, I'm sure he would do, if he learned of it,' Guy Baildon said, in a matter-of-fact tone. 'I had to give your opponent and his friends a fright… but no matter. They're leaving today too. The word is, the King will move up to Honfleur, while Willoughby makes ready to go to Caen. If you hear a noise, it'll be cries of joy from our people. They're going home.'

'God in heaven.' Revill let out a long breath; just then, he could have kissed the fair-faced young messenger on both cheeks. 'So, the order you bring from our muster-master is true, while the one you claimed to carry from the King was a pack of-'

'Steady now,' Baildon broke in. 'I was about to say that you should return to the camp, before they grow suspicious.' He jerked his head towards Dufort and his party, who were looking in their direction. Revill glanced over his shoulder.

'The German – Werner,' he murmured. 'It looks like he and his mercenaries are leaving already. I wasn't sure why they were here in the first place.'

'He's Swiss, not German,' Baildon said. 'And I've no notion, either. Mayhap Dufort paid him – that's all they care about it, isn't it? Swiss pikemen even changed sides at Arques, because they hadn't been paid. Went over to the League – did you hear about that?'

'I did,' Revill answered. 'But now, I'll take your advice and get back to my gunners…' he almost smiled, thinking how relieved Tom Bright would be. 'You'd be welcome to join us for a mug, if there's time?'

At that, the other shook his head. 'We will talk, you and I,' he said. 'Indeed, we must do so – but alone. I have some news. Shall we say, in half an hour?'

'News, for me?' Revill found himself frowning. 'What kind of-'

He was cut short as, with a wave of his hand, Baildon turned sharply away from him. As he went he spoke loudly in French, telling Revill to report to his commander at once; the words, of course, were meant to be overheard by Dufort and his party. So, with a final glance at the man who had put a stop to the duel, but had now mystified him, Revill called out his thanks and stepped away, out of the clearing and into the trees.

But his mind was busy: what kind of news could this quick-witted young fellow be carrying?

**

The next hours were ones of near-frantic activity.

Eager to quit Falaise, this otherwise quiet little town over which they had fought a grim battle, the English forces were losing no time in packing their equipment and dismantling the tents; or at least, those that were worth saving. Since the order to march had been given, the camp was now a heaving mêlée of soldiers, animals and baggage carts, the air filled with the whinnying of horses and the shouts of men. When Revill approached the gun crew's area, he saw that the barrels of Fiery Moll and Spiky Bess had already been covered with sailcloth, while powder and ball, buckets and tools were ready to be loaded onto wagons. But some distance before them, in a body, his crew stood waiting – and the relief that swept over them, at sight of their gun-master walking out of the morning haze unscathed, was as plain as sunlight.

'By Jesus, Captain.' Unable to contain himself, Tom Bright hurried forward and would have hugged him like a brother, barely restraining himself at the last moment. 'We feared... I mean, I feared...' he broke off, almost in tears. 'And with all the excitement and folk running about, I didn't know what to think - but we're going home! What joy, eh?'

Revill managed a nod, then stiffened. The looks on the faces of his men – especially that of dour Dan Newcome – told a rather different tale, he thought.

'You told them, didn't you,' he said, meeting his corporal's eye. 'About my engagement?'

'I had to,' Bright admitted. 'It was my fault, after all... I must have looked so glum, they wormed it out of me.' He looked round briefly. 'Dan was all for knocking me to the ground, while the others were for haring off to the wood after you. I told them you wouldn't like it, but-'

'Well, enough,' Revill interrupted, with some embarrassment. 'No-one's hurt. It's over – indeed, it barely got started. A message came about the march, and... well, shall we put it behind us? There's more than enough to do now, is there not?'

'Aye...' Bright nodded, and heaved a sigh. 'It's... see now, I couldn't have lived with myself, Captain. That is, if...' He fell silent.

Revill clapped him on the shoulder, and turned to the rest of the crew. 'All's well, lads,' he said, with forced cheerfulness.

The others, who had been exchanging looks, now showed only renewed relief. Even Dan Newcome wore a half-smile, while the younger ones grinned. Disaster, it seemed, had been averted, and the march to the coast loomed – and this time neither cold, wind or rain would dampen their spirits. As they began to move off to their tasks, Tom Bright gestured to Revill to come to the crew's tent.

'I've been saving a flagon I got from a French sutler,' he said. 'It's all he would sell me – red wine, rough as old leather. But you'd like a wet, wouldn't you?'

'Well, perhaps I would,' Revill allowed. 'You'll be taking down the tents soon after, then?' But when Bright shrugged, he understood. 'No... why should you? Let's leave them to rot, shall we? It can't be much more than two days' march to Caen - I'd rather share my horse's blanket, and sleep in the cold.'

'My sentiments too, Captain,' the corporal said, brightening again. 'I'll bet you wish it was Malachi, don't you? Instead of that army nag.'

Revill did indeed miss the old warhorse he had been obliged to leave behind, stabled in London. But as the two of them walked towards the tent, a voice called from nearby. He looked round, remembering that the envoy Guy Baildon wished to speak with him. But the man approaching was someone else entirely: the Swiss Captain, Werner, who had stood in the forest clearing to observe the duel. Puzzled, Revill waited.

'Who's this?' Bright muttered, suddenly suspicious.

With more than a trace of unease himself, Revill allowed the man to draw near. Werner halted, made a brief half-bow, then spoke. His English was slow, and Revill thought to suggest they conversed in French - but for some reason, he did not. There was a look in the other's eye that he mistrusted: this was not, he decided, a courtesy visit.

'Master Revill, will you hear me?' He began. 'I am Jannes Werner, captain of-'

'I know,' Revill broke in. 'And I confess I'm surprised by your coming. I have little time, now that we're leaving.'

'I understand,' the man nodded. 'We, however... our company, that is... we are not.'

'Indeed?' Revill met his eye. On a sudden, Guy Baildon's words from but a short time ago flew to his mind: how Swiss pikemen had changed sides at the battle of Arques because they had not been paid, and gone over to the enemy. Somewhat tense, he waited.

'Our service to the King is ending, I should say,' Werner went on. 'For truth, some say he never valued us... but no matter. We will move east. Where there is war, there is opportunity.' Abruptly the man's gaze shifted towards Tom Bright, who stood near with arms folded. Meanwhile, the bustle of the camp went on around them.

'I have a plan... an offer,' the Swiss captain said. 'But it is for your ears alone. After, you will perhaps put it to your men.' He nodded in Bright's direction, making it clear that he wished him to leave.

'My corporal stays,' Revill said at once.

The other paused, then: 'So be it. But I ask that you swear him to be private, as I ask you also to be private when I speak my offer. It is between us, and no-one else.'

'By God,' Revill muttered; now, he understood what he had already suspected. *An offer*, the man had said – and it was plain enough what he meant.

'You want to buy me – and my men too,' he said harshly. 'You want us to turn free lances, and serve the enemy! Is that what you and your soldiers are planning to do: join the Duc de Mayenne's forces and fight for the *liguers* – in effect, for the interests of Spain?'

But hearing that, Captain Werner merely sighed; he appeared to be making an effort to choose his words. After throwing a glance at Bright, he faced Revill again.

'Do you not know how much English gunners are prized?' He asked sharply. 'Through all of Europe, I mean – even as far away as the land of the Great Turk? Englishmen serve in the Sultan's armies – serve a barbarian. Why? Because he pays well – as would Mayenne. You're a soldier, who lives by fighting. This is a dirty war – and a war between Frenchmen too. The people here hate you, as they hate all Englishmen. And do you think Henri of Navarre cares a button for his English allies - that he will thank you, when he has taken Paris and gained the throne? He will forget you, sir – as he will forget your Queen and the aid she has given him. So... yes, you are right. That is what I offer: join me and my soldiers, and fight for gain. Why should you not?'

Revill stood rigid, without expression. A part of him was surprised at how Captain Werner had managed to make such a speech in his halting English; it was almost as if he had learned it. Then he wondered if that were indeed the case, and whether he and his crew were not the only English soldiers the man had tried to recruit. For a while, he waited to see whether he had anything further to add – then he acted.

'You can go to the devil, Werner,' he snapped, dropping a hand to his sword-hilt. 'Take your whoreson offer – that amounts to treason in my eyes – and stuff it down your gullet. I'm no traitor - I serve Elizabeth my Queen, and the King who considers her his ally. As for my men...' He turned deliberately to Tom Bright, and signalled to him to step close.

'Did you get all of that?' He asked.

'Every word, Captain,' Bright grunted - and at his manner and expression, Werner took an involuntary step back. Angrily, he eyed Revill.

'I asked for private talk,' he said. 'I see this man is of your mind - but what of the others? Will you not allow them to take their own decision?'

'Aye, let's do that – *sir*,' Bright said to him at once. 'With your permission, Captain?' And before Revill could reply he turned, put a hand to his mouth and bellowed.

'Newcome, Lambert, Kitto – both Kittos! Over here, and quick!'

There followed an answering shout, and Lam Bowen appeared from behind the tent. The others arrived too, from various directions. No sooner had they gathered than their corporal gestured at Captain Werner, and spoke in a voice of sarcasm.

'You should hear this,' he announced. 'The gentleman here - a Switzer - has made an offer to Captain Revill, to me and to all of you: leave Lord Willoughby's service, and join him and his mercenaries in fighting for the League – against King Henri, that is. Good money, it seems - and no doubt plenty of booty too, if you're not fussy how you get it. He wants an answer quick, so what'll it be? Speak up!'

With that Bright turned to Revill as if he expected a rebuke, but there was none. Instead, as the crew reacted in mingled surprise and unease, their captain raised a hand.

'That's the nub of it, you cannoneers,' he said. 'It's your choice. I'm with Willoughby, for Caen and home - but anyone who wants to leave the company can do so. Though of course…' this with a hard look in Werner's direction: 'The guns belong to the Tower of London – the Queen's armoury. They're not for sale… unless anyone has a notion of how to separate them from the column, when we march? Mayhap the captain here would assist.'

There followed a taut silence – but if doubt had arisen for a moment, it was soon gone. A growl rose among the watching gunners, and it came from Dan Newcome.

'He wants us to turn, does he?' He muttered. 'Switch sides, easy as that? After what we've been through… seen fellow Englishmen die before our eyes?' Taking a step forward he spat heavily, his spittle landing barely a yard from Werner's boots. The Swiss jerked as if struck.

'There's my answer,' Newcome told him, putting a hand to his poniard's hilt for good measure. Glancing round, he eyed his fellows. 'What say you, lads?'

'I say we invite the gentleman for a parley,' Martin Kitto said. But when the others turned sharply, he added: 'I mean a parley from which he doesn't return. Perhaps someone poking about the camp will find him, after we've gone… he might even get a decent burial.'

'I'll go along with that,' the younger Kitto said. Coming forward to stand beside his brother, he scowled at the mercenary. Lam Bowen followed, wearing a similar expression.

'Can we not help the gentleman on his way with a few good kicks, Corporal?' He enquired lightly, to which Bright did not reply. Seeing how matters were moving, however, Revill quickly put himself between his men and Werner, who was now as tense as a wrestler.

'You've had our decision - sir,' he said. 'Don't let us detain you any longer.'

Werner met his eye and might have spoken, but seemed to think better of it - whereupon, as a new thought struck him, Revill added a postscript.

'See now, is that why you were in the wood earlier – to see who won the bout?' He demanded. 'To know whether I would still be alive, for you to come with your offer?' He let out a breath. 'Mayhap you had your eye on the culverins and their crew all along, no matter whether their gun-master was alive or not - is that the measure of it?'

But his words, spoken in indignation, were wasted. With a muttered oath Werner drew back from the group, his gaze sweeping across them where they stood: a solid body, who would yield to no-one.

'Such fine principles,' he snapped. 'And now, I wonder if it was more than mere good fortune that the duel was stopped – eh, Revill? Perhaps you had some arrangement with the messenger, to save you having to fight? I swear, I had not thought to find a coward among the English!'

To that, the gunners reacted with sudden anger, but Revill stayed them. Taking a step forward, he might have struck Werner had not the man veered away. Turning, with a hand on his own sword, he merely spoke a few harsh words and stalked off. Since the parting shot was in German, however, and Swiss German at that, its impact was lost. With a snort, Dan Newcome turned his back on the departing figure and eyed Tom Bright.

'Rumour has it you've been hiding a jug of wine, Corporal,' he said. 'Seems to me, the least you could do is share it with the rest of us before we leave.'

Bright, who had watched Werner until he disappeared among the tents, turned with a frown. 'Well... with the captain's permission, I might,' he grunted.

But the tension was gone, and the men breathed easier. A few grins appeared, then faded as all eyes went to Revill: the captain's mind, it seemed, was suddenly elsewhere. As the others followed his gaze, they saw a lone horseman approaching, and stirred anew.

'Of course – go with the corporal, and drink,' Revill said, turning abruptly to them. 'I'll speak with this messenger... it's likely nothing of import. I'll join you anon – and save a mouthful for me,' he added, forcing a smile.

But as the others moved off towards their tent, his smile faded. Somewhat quickly, he walked forward to meet Guy Baildon, who drew rein at his approach. The young man then dismounted, and lost little time in revealing the news that he had kept for the past half hour – news which sent Revill's spirits plummeting.

It wasn't only mercenaries, it transpired, along with assorted freebooters and glory-hunters, who were to remain behind in France.

To his dismay, so was Captain Will Revill.

THREE

'You'd best read this letter,' Baildon told him, the two of them standing beside his horse, some distance from the encampment. His manner was grave, as if he took no pleasure in his errand. Revill looked down at the folded paper which the other had produced from his coat. A dozen questions had come to mind – but when he saw the seal, his heart sank.

'Heneage,' he muttered, almost to himself. 'By heaven, am I never to be beyond his reach – even on a field of battle?'

Baildon made no reply, but merely held out the letter until Revill took it. Stepping aside, he broke the seal, opened it and read - only to react in sudden fury, which startled the messenger.

'The whoreson rat! I'd like to wring his be-ruffed and bejewelled neck!'

The younger man dropped his gaze, and remained silent.

'How much do you know of this?' Revill demanded, turning on him. 'In fact, who in blazes are you? Odd that I never saw you before today... whom do you serve, Baildon? Answer me!'

'Your answer lies there,' Baildon replied, nodding at the paper. 'If you'd care to finish reading.'

Drawing a breath, Revill forced himself to read the entire letter, before lowering it in near despair. For the past months, caught up as he was in King Henri's war, he had almost managed to put the spymaster out of mind; now, everything came back in a rush of mingled anger and gloom. The cruel hold Sir Thomas Heneage had over him – his ability to threaten Revill's younger sister, who had married a Papist and converted – fell upon him like a dead weight, as did the orders he had given Revill when they last met: to keep a watch on his fellow Englishmen, and report any sign of treachery or disloyalty, or even of disillusion. The last of these could almost make him laugh: after the hardships they had borne, every surviving pikeman, harquebusier and horseman in the army bore disillusion like a badge. As for their commanders, he had seen no sign of anything worse from them than a simple desire to leave this war-torn country and go home. But for Heneage, of course, it was never enough: the man's deep suspicion, shared with Secretary Walsingham, of the slightest hint of a threat to the Queen's safety – real or imagined – ruled him utterly.

But now came a further blow, which Revill read with near-disbelief. Not only, it seemed, was the Vice-Chamberlain disappointed by the lack of reports coming back from France: he was dissatisfied with Revill's cavalier attitude to his assignment. He was issuing new orders, to be carried out without question: Revill was to leave Lord Willoughby's service at once, and work closely with the person who would deliver this letter. Finally, Heneage delivered a sharp reminder to him to remember his position, and not to return until he had carried out the mission. Once again, Revill realised, recalling their very first meeting last autumn, he was being given no choice but to obey.

With a bleak look, he raised his eyes to meet Baildon's.

'So... you're another of his lackeys. And I suppose you use a false name?'

'That's not your concern,' came the reply. 'And since you ask, until now I've only carried despatches. This one left London ten days ago – and the orders came as a surprise to me, too.'

'The *mission*, you mean? Well now, what in God's name am I – are we – supposed to do here? Arrange an unpleasant accident for someone, or-'

'Not here,' Baildon broke in, shaking his head. 'I'll speak further tomorrow, when we leave. Meanwhile, you'll have to concoct a tale for your men. Sir John Burgh and his regiment are staying behind to support the King... you might say you've received orders to join him.'

'What, without guns or gunners?' Revill retorted. 'What use would I be then? My men aren't stupid enough to believe-'

'I leave it to you,' the messenger interrupted, showing impatience at last. 'I'll meet you soon after first light, on the road to the east. It's a long ride, so you need to be ready.'

'Where are we going?'

'To Paris. And you'd best shed anything that smacks of soldiering – you're a private gentleman now. I have a new name for you, but it can wait until we're on our way.'

Whereupon Guy Baildon - despatch-rider and now, it seemed, spy on overseas service for the Queen's Council – turned away and put foot to stirrup.

Revill watched him ride off, standing alone in the muddy field. Just then, he felt as lonely as he had ever felt in his life.

***

That afternoon, when the great cavalcade of foot soldiers, horsemen, wagons and guns at last set off on their journey to Caen, Revill took a bleak farewell of his crew.

He had already had conference with his commander, Lord Willoughby, and had been dreading it. But around eighty English gentlemen, it turned out, along with a handful of others, had already chosen to stay with King Henri for various reasons. Willoughby accepted the matter calmly: he had lost many soldiers and officers, including some close to him, and was as exhausted as any man Revill had seen. But when they shook hands, the courageous young Lord's grip was firm to the last: with a heavy heart, his master of gunnery had left his tent and stepped out into the cold, wishing to heaven he was going home with him.

His final act, after he had made a brief and, to his mind, unconvincing explanation to his gunners, was to see them off with their mounted escort, trailing behind Fiery Moll and Spiky Bess.

Tom Bright, of course, had taken it the hardest; nor did he believe a single word Revill tried to say to him in private, before addressing the rest of the crew.

'You know me better than that.' Bright spoke with bitterness. 'He's got you by the cods again, has he not? I mean Heneage... more dirty business, eh? Where to this time?'

'Don't ask, Tom,' Revill had said finally. 'Just keep your hopes up that I'll be back home by springtime, and we can get drunk at the Three Cranes in the Vintry. I mean proper, falling-down drunk – and I'm paying. Will you do that for me? Along with keeping up the crew's spirits, now you're chief cannoneer?'

'I'll try... but by Jesus, Captain, is there no remedy? Can't you say you're sick, like half the army is? Or better still, you got wounded at Falaise... we could make it look real. I'll even cut your leg open, if it helps.'

But when Revill merely shook his head, his corporal looked deflated. It was as plain as a pikestaff: the captain was leaving him, because he could do no other.

Now, mounted on his army horse, Revill chose to ride a half mile or so with his men, to see them on their way before turning back. The mood of the crew, of elation at their impending return, was tempered with sadness. They were like a family, who had come through fire, blood and mayhem and managed to survive – but now, one of them

35

was quitting. As they trudged behind the two culverins, hauled by their teams of packhorses, each man voiced his regret. The last word came from Dan Newcome, who came up beside Revill's stirrup and gave one of his snorts.

'How will you fadge, sir, without me and the others to run around after you?' He demanded. 'It's folly, that's what. Supposing your orders had come a day late – even a few hours late? You'd be on your way with us now, wouldn't you?'

'I suppose so,' Revill allowed. 'And no man wishes it more than I. I'll even miss your griping… you're too old for soldiering, Newcome. Back to London with you, and stay there.'

With a sigh, he leaned down and offered his hand, which the other seized. Then he was gone, moving back to the main body. The rest of the crew paused to call out their farewells as Revill turned his mount and, with a final wave, left them. His last glimpse was of Bright, head down as he trudged away.

When he got back to what remained of the gunners' camp, he looked inside the crew's ragged tent to make sure that all had been cleared. Just beyond the entrance was a stoneware flagon, with a scrap of paper tied to the neck. When he lifted it, he found that the vessel was still almost a quarter full, while the paper bore a few words scrawled in a clumsy, soldier's hand:

'*Finish, and drink to us.*'

Revill drank, and though the blood-red wine was as Tom Bright had said - as rough as old leather - he did not stop until he had drained the last drop.

***

The following morning, dressed in plain garb, he sat his horse on the road east of Falaise and waited until Guy Baildon came cantering up, drew rein with gloved hands, and nodded towards the thoroughfare ahead.

'We'll speak as we ride,' he said.

Wordlessly, Revill eased his mount forward. The old army nag, as Bright had described it, was indeed past its youth, but bore its latest master stoically enough. His caliver hung at one side of the saddle in its scabbard, his pack on the other. In a poor humour, having slept fitfully in his old tent while a cold wind blew through it, he was in no mood for conversation; his new companion, however, had much to say.

'You must remember that I'm now a Frenchman,' he announced. 'Don't slip into English with me, whatever you do. If someone says something you don't understand, pretend you're hard of hearing. And my name is Castillon - Jean Castillon. You, however, will remain an Englishman. Your name's Thomas Perrot. We're emissaries from the Duc de Mayenne.'

At which, Revill's jaw dropped.

'We're *what*?'

'Emissaries, from the Catholic League. We've been sent to meet with the English ambassador, Sir Edward

37

Stafford.' But seeing that his companion had reined in and was gazing at him with incredulity, Baildon sighed and drew his own horse to a halt.

'I know who Stafford is,' Revill told him harshly. 'But as for posing as an emissary from Mayenne - a Papist?' He shook his head. 'It's a fool's errand. You might bluff it, but I'd be arrested as a spy before I'd even got through the gates of Paris!'

'You would not,' came the sharp reply. 'You can leave the talking to me, until we're safe in our lodging. Another will meet us there – a Frenchman. He will lead us to the ambassador's residence, in the Faubourg St Germain. Thereafter, a man of your abilities should be able to convince Sir Edward of the truth – not to say, the importance - of our mission.' He paused. 'Indeed, my master in London has assured me that you must do so, Revill - for I was told that you have no other choice. And by the way, that is the last time I'll use your real name. So, Master Perrot - shall we ride on?'

But Revill remained where he was, angry and silent. There was something odd about Baildon, he decided, though just now he could not think what it was. Was the man even who he claimed to be? In the world of intelligencers, few things were plain or simple. Heneage's letter, however, was genuine. But as for the order – to pose as Catholic envoys on urgent business with the English ambassador... he shook his head.

'See now, if I'm English but supposed to be sent by Mayenne, then I'm a damned traitor,' he retorted. 'One of those Papists who serves Spain – like that devil Stanley, the governor of Deventer, who betrayed it to the enemy and turned. I can't do it, I'm telling you – and besides, I say it again: even if I tried, I'd be discovered at once.'

'Not if you try hard enough,' the other returned. 'Don't you see? Your presence will serve to convince the ambassador that our offer is real. Even if he were suspicious of us, he's more likely to believe a fellow Englishman.' His expression hardening, he drew a sharp breath. 'But as I've said, you have no choice. You must aid me.'

A moment passed. His mind whirling, Revill searched for further argument, but his case was hopeless. Briefly, he pictured Sir Thomas Heneage the last time he had seen him... the man's fine clothes, and his wry smile; not for the first time, he cursed the Vice-Chamberlain from the bottom of his heart. And yet there was nothing for it, he saw, but to relent and to work with Baildon – or Jean Castillon, as he must now call him.

It felt like a betrayal... or a surrender, as bitter as any he had known.

'So, what's the reason for our visit to Stafford?' He asked finally. 'And this offer, whatever it is - what makes you so sure we would be believed?'

'Of course, that is essential to our mission,' Baildon said. But growing impatient, he frowned. 'See now, the details must wait. A two-day ride to Paris lies ahead of us, and I want to reach Evreux by nightfall. We'll find an inn, and there I'll explain more. But now I'm getting cold, so…'

And with that, he dug heels to the flanks of his horse, which sprang forward. Revill could only follow, squinting into the pale sun which rose ahead. At least, he thought, he was not being ordered to assassinate anyone.

And thankfully, the weather seemed to be holding off.

***

They were late in reaching the town of Evreux, which bestrode a crossroads on the old road southwards from Rouen, where it traversed the great highway to Paris. Night had fallen, and the two had not spoken for hours. When they arrived at the gates, however, in spite of himself Revill was impressed by Baildon's mastery of vernacular French, along with his powers of persuasion. Producing a written pass from inside his coat - which no-one could have read clearly by lantern-light – Monsieur Castillon, as he now was, convinced the guards that he was on state business, and not to be thwarted. Whereupon, after only a short delay, the two of them were permitted to ride forward into the cobbled streets, where they stopped at the first inn they saw. Having dismounted and entrusted their horses to the stableman, they paused at the doorway.

'Remember, I'm French - and it's an *auberge*, not a tavern,' Baildon said. Too tired, hungry and saddle-sore to utter a riposte, Revill followed him inside.

The place was busy, and there was only one small chamber available. Having taken supper in silence, paid for by Baildon, they retired to the room and lit a candle. The younger man sat down on the only stool, while Revill stretched out on one of the straw-filled pallets.

'I've a mind to sleep,' he muttered. 'Whatever you've got to tell me, can't it wait until morning?'

'I'd rather get it said now,' the other replied. 'Then you can sleep on it.' He was as tired as Revill, but struck him as being somewhat on edge. He had brought a cup of wine upstairs with him, from which he took a drink. He offered it to Revill but was met with refusal, at which he shrugged, then began to speak rapidly.

'Sir Edward Stafford, who's been Her Majesty's ambassador here these past six years and more: in short, the man isn't trusted. He was too friendly with the Duke of Guise once – then he got close to a Spaniard named Mendoza. There's a suspicion he passed intelligence to Mendoza, which found its way to Madrid. I'm talking about events of two years back – you'll recall what was about to be unleashed, just then.'

Revill barely nodded; no-one needed reminding of the Armada.

'The fact is, Stafford was supposed to supply Walsingham with intelligence about the Spanish fleet, but he failed to do so,' Baildon went on. 'Sir Francis was angry, but there was no proof of treachery - the ambassador's a gambler, and often short of money. He's accepted loans from Papists – even from Guise too, we heard. He's weak, and a weak ambassador is something England cannot afford. Not here, not now - not ever. I assume you agree?'

He raised his brows, and waited.

'I don't understand,' Revill objected. 'With all that you've said, why hasn't the Queen merely recalled him? Replaced him with a man of proven loyalty?'

'Well, there's the rub,' came the reply. 'Stafford is close with Lord Burghley. He was never a friend to Walsingham - and as I said, there was no proof of treason. Heneage thinks some of the intelligence Spain received in recent years was incorrect – it could even be that Stafford stayed loyal, and fed them false tidings. It's all, shall we say, a bit muddled.'

'And so, I suppose someone must sound the ambassador out,' Revill said with a frown. 'Test his loyalty…' On a sudden, he sat up. 'Wait – you're not telling me that's *my* task?'

Baildon met his eye. 'Not entirely,' he answered. 'Once we arrive at-'

'By the Christ, you are!' Rising from the pallet, Revill stood over him. 'That's work for an agent – one of Walsingham's best men,' he exclaimed. 'I've told you already, I'd be found out. If Stafford's a traitor, he'd smell deception from the start. As for my posing as a renegade…' Throwing his arms up, he let them fall helplessly. 'The scheme is mad – and Heneage should know better. I might almost think he's laid this on me deliberately so I'll end up dead, floating in the Seine...'

But he broke off: with infuriating calmness, Baildon was taking another sip from his cup. Having done so, he lowered it and let out a breath.

'To begin with, as I've explained, you will not be alone,' he said. 'The one who'll take the role of chief emissary – his name, as far as you need know, being Etienne – knows his part perfectly. You are there merely to add weight to the matter. At the right moment, you'll reveal yourself as a fellow Englishman, and confirm Mayenne's offer. Money, of course, will be a major part of it... but I'll leave it to Etienne to tell you more. For all I know, matters may have moved on since I was last in Paris.'

'Oh?' Revill threw him a dour look. 'When was that, then?'

But the other showed his impatience. 'I'm growing tired of your questions,' he said, before giving a yawn. 'You don't trust me – why would you? I'm not inclined to trust you either – Master Perrot. But we serve the same Queen, do we not? And we've been tasked with a mission of importance – it may even be vital to the war. Isn't that enough?'

Revill made no reply. His mind was a fog - a jumble of thoughts which might well keep him from the rest he badly needed. Letting out a sigh, he slumped down on his pallet. There he pulled off his boots, coat and breeches, and finally lay down. His companion, meanwhile, stretched out fully clothed on the other pallet, pulled the coverlet over himself and turned his face to the wall. And that was exactly how Revill found him the following morning, when he finally awoke from a deep, if troubled sleep.

It looked as if the young despatch carrier-turned-intelligencer had never moved, all night.

***

The ride to Paris, more than fifty miles along a busy road, passed in near silence and without event. Stopping only to water the horses and to buy bread along the way, to be consumed as they rode, the two men often kept apart, in single file. By the time dusk had fallen both were stiff and weary as well as taut with anticipation, and not even Baildon bothered to hide it. Drawing his mount alongside Revill's, he spoke up.

'We're but a mile or so from the city,' he announced, as if his fellow-traveller had failed to notice the increasing number of farms and cottages. 'When we approach the gate – the Porte St Honore – we'll dismount. As at Evreux, I'll speak for us both...' he frowned. 'For now, it's best you pose as my servant: hold the horses, and act respectful.'

'I thought I was supposed to be Thomas Perrot – as English as roast beef,' Revill muttered sourly. It was more than irritability on his part, he knew: it was plain hostility. Paris was a stronghold of the Catholic League, who defied Henri IV and refused to accept him as king: the very people, in fact, whom he had been fighting for months.

44

'Once we're at the lodgings you can be as you like,' Baildon retorted. 'Unless, that is, you truly want to get arrested. Moreover, our difficulties won't cease once we're inside-'

'No, they're just beginning,' Revill broke in. 'Supposing my clothing arouses comment, or my caliver? It may as well have "English-made" stamped on it - as could my boots.'

'Will you cease cavilling?' The other snapped. 'I got us into Evreux, and I'll get us into Paris. Now, if you'll allow me, I'll ride ahead.' He shook the reins and moved forward.

With a silent oath, Revill followed suit. The lights of dwellings went by, more and more of them lining the road that led to the west gate. Away to his left, he glimpsed windmills on a mount, then a bridge across a moat appeared, lit by torches – and finally the gate itself loomed, its arch towering overhead. Slowing the horses to a walk, the two riders passed through a handful of people. Parisian-accented French filled Revill's ears, as a foul reek from the moat assailed his nostrils. Before him lay the largest city in Europe; to him, its very walls looked forbidding enough.

When Baildon halted, he stopped and dismounted stiffly. And soon, in an echo of yesterday's moment of tension at the gates of Evreux, he was listening once again to Monsieur Jean Castillon explain to the heavily-armed guards how important it was that he and his servant were admitted, on matters of state. This time, however, as he stood holding the horses' reins, his relief at the other's success was somewhat greater. Only when he found himself in a wide, bustling thoroughfare, which he would learn was the Grande Rue St Honore, did he begin to breathe easier. Finally, after Baildon had waited for him to catch up, he stopped beside him.

'Are you content now?' His companion enquired, with a look of scorn. 'Or do you still think I'm little more than a youth, who's in waters too deep for him?'

'Not at all - I'm filled with admiration,' Revill told him. 'And if the lodgings you spoke of are even half-decent, I'll likely fall at your feet in gratitude. So, which direction is it?'

Without bothering to reply the other turned, took his horse's reins from him and prepared to mount. And a half hour later, having crossed the Seine to the island with its great cathedral, then crossed by another bridge to the south bank, they reached the Faubourg St Germain. Whereupon, after threading their way through a number of narrow streets, they stopped at last outside a small, low-roofed house. Revill peered at the unlit windows, thinking he could almost sleep in the saddle.

In fact, to his relief the night would prove to be one of comfort. What the morning would bring, however - let alone the coming days - he could not have imagined.

FOUR

He awoke in a narrow, low-ceilinged chamber, with the sound of rain thudding on the roof, and sat up with a jolt. He had thought he was in his tent, back at the Falaise camp... then as memory returned, he fell back upon the pillow. A moment later he looked round, and realised he was alone. The other bed, a rope structure that sagged as his did, and where Baildon had slept, was now empty.

He sat up again and tried to recall their arrival the previous evening, both of them so saddle-sore and weary they desired only sleep. He vaguely remembered settling the horses in a dingy stable nearby. Then he remembered a woman in a plain hood, who had lit the way up a narrow stairway with a candle. A jug of water had been placed on the floor of the room, along with a platter of bread and cheese, which both men fell upon as soon as she left them. Then, without further word, they had lain down and slept.

Now, from the light that came through a single window, Revill saw that it was long past dawn. Finding his clothes piled on the floor where he had left them, he dressed quickly, opened the door and ventured downstairs. He found himself in a large but humble room, with one door wedged slightly open to the street, and another leading out the back. Across the room a log fire burned. As he left the stair, someone appeared from the rear doorway.

'*Monsieur… vous m'avez effrayé…*'

'*Pardon, madame.*' Gathering himself, Revill spoke in French, apologising for startling the woman: the same one, he realised, who had admitted him and Baildon the night before. He saw a small, comely figure of somewhat less than forty years, clad in a blue frock with black hair tucked under her hood. At sight of him she had put hand to mouth, but now lowered it. A short silence followed, before Revill enquired about his companion, Monsieur Castillon – only to receive a shock.

He had gone, the woman told him, saying nothing about whether he would return.

'But we have… we had business,' he muttered. 'What the devil does he…'

He caught his breath: he had spoken English, as he had feared he might do from the very start of this enterprise. But when he glanced sharply at the householder, he received a surprise: instead of showing alarm, she relaxed.

'So, you are *Anglais*,' she said. 'I should have guessed.'

'You understood me?' Uneasily, Revill glanced towards the street door, beyond which the rain fell in torrents. 'Perhaps I should explain.'

'Better not, monsieur,' came the reply. Taking a step forward, his hostess – for so she appeared to be – gestured him to a small table. A pitcher of milk stood upon it, alongside a platter heaped with hunks of bread and a pot of preserves. 'Better you eat first.'

'Well, then I thank you…' His mind busy, he took one of two nearby stools and sat himself down. 'Might I know your name?'

'I am Elise Bodin,' came the reply.

'I'm… Thomas Perrot,' Revill told her. 'A friend to Monsieur Castillon. We came from-'

'Please – eat,' Elise Bodin repeated, with a touch of impatience. 'While you do so, I will speak.' Coming round the table, she lifted the pitcher and poured milk into a mug. In silence he took it up, nodded his thanks and drank.

'Your business, Monsieur Perrot – it is not my concern,' she said, folding her arms. 'We should tell each other nothing. I will say only that you are safe. Like my husband, who no longer lives, I am Huguenot and will not betray you. Soon you will be gone - until then, rest here and wait. Besides, the rain forbids walking.'

Revill met her eye, and saw… what? Strength, and intelligence, along with what might have been an underlying sadness. But he had a picture, of sorts: she was a widow and a Protestant, who appeared to live alone. Though how she came to speak English was a mystery.

'Wait? Well… I am supposed to meet with someone here,' he said finally.

'Etienne,' Madame Bodin nodded. 'He will come today, or tomorrow… I cannot say.'

'You know him?' He asked, only to receive a shrug.

'A little. Now – *assez, monsieur.*' And she would have moved away, but stopped herself. 'I know you are wary of me,' she added. 'But I say again, you may stay without fear. As for my English speech: I was in London once.'

With a nod, Revill found his tension easing; he managed a polite smile - the first one he had given, he realised, in days. The widow, however, turned and went off through the rear door.

And after that he ate breakfast at leisure, remembering that he had pipe and tobacco in his pack upstairs. Let the rain fall, he thought; thus far, things could have been worse.

***

The day passed, with no sign of the man Etienne, and by evening he had grown fretful.

Despite the tranquillity of the house, where no visitors came and the hostess went about her daily business calmly, unease enveloped him. The rain had stopped after mid-day, and people passed by outside, the distant rumble of the great city reminding him of London. But a nagging doubt was upon him, concerning Baildon's abrupt departure without warning. What, now, should he think? He had gained the impression that Baildon, as Castillon, along with Revill himself and this man Etienne, were to go to the English ambassador's house in a body… had he misunderstood? He knew that he was to pose as a Catholic who had turned traitor to his Queen, and that Etienne would brief him further - but even Elise Bodin, it seemed, was uncertain when the man would arrive. Moreover, what was her involvement? He had heard rumours that the French, unlike the English, used female spies; the thought merely added to his unease. Had she even given him her true name?

At supper-time, when his hostess surprised him by joining him at table, he had a notion to try and discover more, but her manner made him think better of it. While they ate – an excellent mutton stew, and the best meal Revill had eaten in months – the woman kept silent. There was a jug of watered wine on the table, which she invited him to share. But he drank sparingly, his senses alert. Night had fallen, and the hum of the city had diminished. After wiping the last of the stew up with a wedge of bread, he pushed his platter aside and murmured his thanks. Madame Bodin merely nodded.

'So, you were in London once,' he said, with a casual air. 'What did you think of the city?'

She too had finished her meal, and glanced at him before lowering her gaze. 'It was a long time ago, monsieur... nowadays, I think not of it.'

'I did not mean to pry,' he went on. 'You surprised me, is all.'

She said nothing - and now, a thought sprang to his mind. She was a Huguenot, and it was less than eighteen years since the terrible massacre of Protestants in Paris, on Saint Bartholomew's day. In 1572 she would have been a young woman, perhaps newly married. Some of those who

managed to escape the slaughter had fled to England…
had she been among them? And what of her husband – had
he escaped too, or even perished? The sadness he believed
she bore… he realised he was gazing at her, and lowered
his eyes.

'Are you sated now, monsieur?'

He looked up and regretted his carelessness, for she was
returning his gaze with some resentment. But then why,
after all, should she trust him? They were alone, and it was
becoming clear that Etienne would not arrive until the
morrow; already the city gates would be shut. Drawing a
breath, he sought for some words of assurance.

'Your pardon, madame,' he murmured. 'I'm indebted to
you already, and after such a meal, my debt is
compounded. I'll go to the chamber where I slept last
night, and greet you in the morning.'

Upon which he rose, inclined his head and was turning
away when she spoke – and this time, there was a warning
in her eyes.

'I would hope so, Monsieur Perrot. Whatever you think,
I have no special regard for Englishmen – and nor, I will
say, does Etienne. I pray you, remember that you are
surrounded by enemies. One word from either of us would
see you taken and thrown into the Bastille Saint-Antoine.
I wish you good-night - but take heed: there is no lock on
your door.'

Revill met her eye, berating himself inwardly; did she
believe that he desired her, and might try to take

advantage? Turning away, he strode to the stairwell and climbed to the upper floor. As he gained the door to his chamber, which indeed had no lock, he saw that there was another door opposite which he had failed to notice. Had he been so befuddled that morning, he wondered? It troubled him briefly... but not as much as the next thought: that he had offended, or even angered, the woman who had given him food and shelter.

And to whom, he now realised, he was foolishly but quite helplessly attracted.

***

He had slept for only a few hours, when he was startled by a sound which made him fling back the coverlet at once.

In the pitch dark he sat up and listened, but heard nothing. Had he merely dreamed? He thought he had heard a thud, yet the house seemed quiet. Nevertheless, he got to his feet and reached for his poniard, which he had placed under the bed. Padding silently to the door in his shirt and hose, he put an ear to it - and tensed immediately.

Someone was moving about downstairs, and trying to keep quiet.

Softly he opened the door. The stairway was dark, but he was certain that the door to Madame Bodin's chamber was closed. He peered downwards and saw a faint glow, which must be the dying embers of the fire.

Poniard in hand, he began a careful descent of the stairs, hoping that none would creak. Thoughts rose in quick succession: were housebreakers as much of a threat in

Paris, he wondered, as they were in London? A woman who lived alone would be an easy target - could she have failed to lock the street door? It seemed unlikely…

He had almost reached the lowest stair when there came a sudden crash, as of breaking crockery. Whereupon, throwing caution aside, he hurried down into the room - and froze.

A tall man in outdoor clothing was standing over the table, stuffing his mouth hungrily with bread. In the fire's glow, Revill glimpsed a pool of some spilled liquid: the intruder must have knocked over a cup. Instinctively he dropped into a half-crouch, as the man gave a start and looked up.

'*Qui est là?*'

Summoning his French, Revill countered by demanding to know who the other was. There was no answer; instead, the fellow stepped quickly away from the table, a hand going to his belt. But when Revill repeated his question there came a snort, and a muttered oath.

'*Anglais…* of course.' The tall man peered at him. 'So, you are here already – Perrot. You must have ridden hard… I almost admire your horsemanship.'

He spoke English well, but with an accent Revill could not place, perhaps from the south of France. Then, as realisation broke, he straightened up and lowered his poniard.

'Etienne?'

'If you like,' came the tart reply. Neither of them moved; Revill saw a faint glimmer of metal, and knew that the other had drawn his own weapon.

'You're correct,' he said. 'I am Perrot. I understood you wouldn't come before the morning... do you have a key?'

But Etienne, it seemed, was not inclined to be conversational. As his eyes adjusted to the light, Revill saw a muscular man with a deeply-lined face framed by long hair. He was scowling, and made no move to sheath his poniard.

'Where is she?' He demanded abruptly, with a glance towards the stairwell.

'Madame Bodin, you mean? I assume she's still abed.'

'So, how long you have stayed here? And where is the other one – Castillon?'

'Castillon left early this morning,' Revill replied. 'As to why he did so, I have no idea. I was hoping you might be able to tell me.'

'You mean, you and she have been alone?' Came the quick reply. 'What did you do?'

'I don't follow,' Revill said sharply. 'If you're implying anything improper-'

'Improper?' The other gave a snort. 'What a feeble word. Then, I should have known they would send me a fool, and an English fool at that. Well, Monsieur Perrot, I ask once more: what have you done here all day – and this night?'

At that, Revill let out a sigh; if this was the man he was supposed to work with, he thought, the two of them had made a most unpromising start. As for Etienne's suspicions – had his hostess not said that she knew the man only slightly?

'What have I done? I merely waited for you,' he said at last. 'I had no way of knowing when you would arrive – even Madame Bodin was unsure. And if this is jealousy on your part, you have no cause for it – none at all.'

A moment passed as they eyed each other; and now, Revill felt only disappointment. This person, he reminded himself, was to lead him to the house of the English ambassador, where they would lay forth a scheme to test the man's loyalty. He had expected a shrewd intelligencer, rather than an ill-tempered fellow with the air of a street bully - whereupon Etienne confounded him by breaking into laughter. The change in his manner was startling: frowning, Revill merely stared.

'*Alors, cela me suffit* – that's good, Master Perrot,' the other said, switching rapidly from French to English. 'I need to have some measure of you. You should go back to your bed now, and we will talk over our breakfast… she's a fine cook, no? Madame Bodin?'

Revill, however, was unsettled: he knew that his first impression of Etienne had sunk home, and would remain. But then, there was no requirement that co-conspirators should like each other; they had their orders, and must see them through. With an effort, he lowered his poniard. Etienne paused, then sheathed his.

At which moment there came a sound from the stairway, and both men looked round quickly. Wrapped in a heavy gown and holding a candle, her hair loose, Elise Bodin stood on the lowest stair, regarding the new arrival without expression.

'Late, as always.' With a sigh, she turned her eyes on Revill. 'So, monsieur... I see I have no need to make introduction. Have you enjoyed your talk? For myself, I would prefer not to be awoken...' She paused. 'Or perhaps you thought a thief had come, and wished to defend me? In which case, bravo. Now I will return to my bed – and I ask only for quiet.'

With that, his hostess turned and began to climb. The candlelight faded, and there followed the noise of a door banging shut.

Revill turned back to Etienne... but that one, it seemed, had dismissed him too. Without a word he took a stool, slumped down at the table with arms extended, and laid his head on them. As Revill ascended the stairs he glanced back, and believed the man was already asleep.

***

When he came down in the morning Etienne was seated at the table, eating what looked like curds from a bowl. Barely looking up, he gestured vaguely. Once again bread and preserves were laid out, along with a pitcher and a dish of fruits. Sitting down opposite him, Revill took bread and plums, and enquired after the hostess.

'At market,' came the terse reply. 'She leaves us to talk.'

'Well then,' he answered, 'I'll leave that to you.'

They took breakfast in silence, while street noises drifted in through the doorway. Once again, Revill noticed, the door had been wedged slightly ajar.

'Why does she leave it like that?' He asked.

Etienne was finishing his meal unhurriedly, but following Revill's eye he glanced round at the door. 'Perhaps she likes to stop anyone gaining entry, yet observe them at the same time. One cannot be too careful… there are rogues everywhere, *non*?'

Mastering his impatience, Revill pushed his platter aside and sat back. He waited for the other to do the same, whereupon they eyed each other.

'So… our esteemed friend, Sir Edward Stafford,' Etienne said, without preamble. 'Once a Member of Parliament, and once a carrier of secret despatches for Lord Burghley… which is how he got himself knighted and appointed ambassador to France. What do you know of him?'

'Only that he's not to be trusted. I was told you would enlighten me further.'

'*Alors*, it's a nice house he has,' the other said, with apparent carelessness. 'On the Quai des Bernardins, close to the river... not that I've ever been inside, of course.'

Revill waited.

'His wife's older than he is… a man might wonder at, shall we say, the suitability of the match,' Etienne continued. 'But there are children, I believe, back in

England. He was in debt, even then. When he married the widow - one of the Howards, no less - her son was not yet of age, so Stafford was hoping to acquire his estate. But he lost... in short, *mon ami*, the man's a fool. Hence, once we've convinced him we're who we claim to be, he should be pliant enough... potter's clay, in our hands.'

'Simple as that, eh?' Revill said dryly.

'Well, we won't have to do all the talking,' came the bland reply. 'The money will do most of that for us. When he hears how much our supposed masters are willing to pay, *monsieur l'ambassadeur* will probably soil his breeches.'

'So, we're to offer him a bribe,' Revill said. Though from what Baildon had told him, he had already guessed that this was the case. 'To do what, precisely?'

'That's obvious, is it not?'

Etienne, he decided, was beginning to irritate him. It was as if the man were explaining the facts to a child. He drew a breath, looked away briefly, then:

'Let's say that it isn't. Let's say that I'd like to hear you spell the whole scheme out, in full. Since I must pose as a traitor – perhaps even gamble my life in the process - I would like to know the odds. Call it folly, if you will - or just a plain man's natural suspicion.'

'Ah... very well.' The other gave a sigh. 'Did Castillon not tell you more about Stafford?'

'He's a gambling man, I understand.'

'He is… and did you know that gambling was forbidden in France?'

Revill indicated that he did not.

'Indeed… the last ban was issued by Henri the Third, as I recall, more than a decade back.'

'So, the ambassador gambles in private?'

'With English exiles… some of them, shall we say, men of dubious character.'

'Rather like us,' Revill said drily. 'Or rather, the sort of men we're pretending to be.'

'If you like,' came the terse reply. 'But whereas I am clearly French - from which Stafford will assume I am Catholic – you, *mon ami*, will have to work a little harder. If he asks, you may say you're one of the turncoats fighting for Stanley in the Low Countries-'

'I know that already,' Revill broke in. 'And I did fight over there – but for our Queen, of course. Hence, I'm not sure I can be convincing as a Papist. You'll have to help me.'

'I will do what I can,' Etienne said shortly. 'But if the man grows suspicious, I mean to withdraw and let you talk to him, as a fellow Englishman. You must use whatever means you can. Walsingham's a dying man, I am told. He will not – he cannot - afford failure. Nor, I expect, can you.' He paused, then: 'We are all at the mercy of our masters in some way, are we not?'

Revill made no reply. It was not Sir Francis Walsingham's displeasure he feared, but that of Sir

Thomas Heneage, who had taken over many of Master Secretary's duties. The memory of his predicament - the cruel hold the Vice-Chamberlain had over him – sprang to his mind like a stab of pain.

'So… I'll put my plan before you now, and after that we shall trust to luck,' Etienne said, growing brisk on a sudden. 'The Quai is not far, and we will walk. Remember – we are emissaries from Mayenne, and must look the part. You should improve your appearance… you look somewhat shabby, Perrot. The widow may have a few clothes still, that belonged to her husband… she's a sentimental woman under it all. A crucifix around your neck would help. I'll pick one up at market when I go out soon. Is there anything else you need?'

Unable to think of anything, Revill shrugged. 'When are we going to the ambassador's house?'

'Did I not say?' Etienne raised his brows. 'This afternoon… we only arrived in Paris today, you understand, and made haste to go directly to him.' Impatiently, he added: 'Do you have more questions, before I instruct you?'

'Just one,' Revill replied, after a moment's pause. He was absorbing the startling fact that the deception was afoot already, and he had little time to ready himself. 'This bribe that we're about to offer Stafford – does it really exist? I mean, if he accepts it-'

'Ah… a fair question,' the other broke in. 'I do not, as you might imagine, carry such a large sum of money about

61

my person. Nevertheless, we must convince him that it exists, and that it could be in his hands very soon if he agrees to our demands. As he surely will… a man of his sort, and in his position, could hardly refuse.'

'And how much is the sum?' Revill asked.

'Fifteen thousand crowns – enough to keep his wife in the manner in which she was once accustomed, before she discovered what a fool she married. Enough to settle his debts too, no doubt, and then gamble on to his heart's content.'

And with that Etienne broke into a sudden laugh, as he had done the evening before. Though there was no mirth in it, Revill saw: only brazen confidence, mingled with a degree of contempt.

He drew a breath, and braced himself for a trying day ahead.

FIVE

In the early afternoon, the two men left the house of Elise Bodin and walked via quiet cobbled streets to the Quai des Bernardins.

The day was chilly and cloudy, with a hint of more rain to come. Revill now wore a plain but good quality doublet borrowed from his hostess; he was fortunate, she had told him, for it was the only one of her late spouse's that she possessed. His own spare breeches, unstained with the mud of Normandy, would serve well enough, as would his sword and the shoes he had taken pains to clean. And as a final touch, helped by the fact that the doublet was slightly too large for him, a small silver crucifix might be seen just below his neck. Beyond that, as Etienne had said, he would simply have to trust to luck.

They did not speak, but made their way through the passers-by, who grew in number when they emerged from a side-street on to the riverside. The Seine, grey and torpid in the dull afternoon, lapped at the stone quays, while across the water the towers of Notre Dame loomed. Revill looked at the row of fine houses lining the Quai des Bernardins, then gave a start as Etienne touched his arm. The ambassador's residence, he murmured, was only a few paces ahead. Moments later they were at the gate to a small, walled garden, and after a brief explanation to a French guard, were admitted.

When the main door was opened, a male servant greeted them. Somewhat to Revill's unease he was English, armed and suspicious. After trying some words of explanation, Etienne turned to his companion and signalled that he should address the man.

'We're here on important business,' Revill said. 'We must see Sir Edward at once.'

'Well then, who should I say is come?' The servant demanded.

'My name's Perrot, and my companion is-'

'*Je suis* Auclair,' Etienne broke in at once. 'Jean Auclair.'

A moment passed, before the other asked the nature of their business - at which, Revill saw, his companion was making an effort to curb his impatience.

'We're, as you say, emissaries from a military leader, *mon ami* – one of the highest of men,' Etienne put in clumsily, as if he were struggling to speak English. 'You will know there is a war, less than a hundred miles from here. But perhaps you have not heard of the King's intentions to march east - towards Paris?'

In spite of everything, Revill had to admire his companion's nerve. For his part, he was too preoccupied with the forthcoming meeting with the ambassador. But he held the servant's gaze, as did Etienne, until the man nodded and said he would conduct them to Sir Edward's private chamber. First, he asked that both of them surrender their swords and poniards, which they agreed to do. Thereafter they followed their guide through the fine, well-furnished house and halted outside a painted door. The servant knocked and went inside, pulling it shut behind him, while the two bogus emissaries stood in silence. After a moment the man reappeared and held the door wide. They entered - then halted as a voice boomed out.

'*Bienvenue, messieurs!*'

The ambassador - a handsome, well-dressed man in his late thirties - was walking towards them wearing a smile of hearty bonhomie. Revill made his bow, while Etienne fell at once into his role as Jean Auclair. From that moment forth, not a word of English would pass his lips.

Sir Edward Stafford spoke French well enough, it became clear, and having gestured the two men to be seated, retreated behind his table. And so, quite quickly, the stratagem was begun. No sooner had Etienne began talking, however, than the ambassador began to frown, and finally raised a hand. What followed then was a stream of rapid French, bouncing back and forth between the two of them, which Revill failed to follow. When at last a pause arose, he turned a questioning eye to his companion.

But Etienne refused to meet his gaze. Instead, he addressed Sir Edward again in an earnest manner, punctuated with smiles and gestures. Finally, Revill caught a name: that of the Duc de Mayenne. Whereupon, without warning, the ambassador turned to Revill and spoke sharply to him in French.

Remaining outwardly calm, Revill hesitated – but before he could summon a reply, Etienne broke in. His trusted friend, he said in French, was an Englishman… perhaps it would be prudent for he himself to withdraw, and let the two of them converse in private?

'By God – you're English?' Sir Edward blurted. 'Why did you not proclaim it? And what did you say your name was?'

'Thomas Perrot, sir,' Revill replied. 'And I too, am come from the Duc de Mayenne.'

A silence followed. The ambassador was frowning again, his eyes shifting between the two of them. Then at last, to the relief of both, he looked at Etienne and gave a nod. With a show of reluctance, Etienne rose, made a brief bow and turned towards the door. As he went, he threw Revill a glance that spoke plainly enough: he was on, and must not fail.

The door closed, Revill turned to face the man – but was stayed at once.

'Slimy bastard,' he muttered. 'I detest the southern French… from Limousin, I'd guess.'

And with that, he leaned back in his chair. 'So – Perrot. Let's hear your embassy. For in truth, I'm somewhat confused. What is it, precisely, that your master desires of me?'

'Has my – has Monsieur Auclair not conveyed it, sir?' Revill enquired. 'While I admit he tends towards somewhat flowery speech, I-'

'Flowery?' Stafford broke in. 'You might say so. But apart from a lot of pleasantries, I've yet to hear the nub of it...' He paused. 'I could do with a drink - will you have one?'

Without waiting for a reply, he rose and went to a side table. Soon a cup appeared, which Revill took while murmuring his thanks. His host sat down, lifted his own cup and drank, then eyed him.

'The wine is from Aquitaine. Never been there myself... I hear it's baking hot. So, Perrot – which part of blessed Albion do you hail from?'

'Well, in truth it's a long time since I left my home,' Revill answered, thinking fast. 'I've been so long abroad, I-'

'Nonsense,' the other broke in. 'I know a West Country accent when I hear it. Devon, is it?'

'You have a good ear, sir,' Revill said, managing a smile. 'Devon it is.'

The other smiled slightly and drank again, then: 'Have you been in London lately? I'm always eager for tidings... the despatches I get take far too long.'

'I confess I've not been there in a while,' Revill answered.

'I'm told Walsingham is dying, and hardly leaves his bed. Do you know aught of that?'

'No more than you, sir. The last I heard, he's not expected to live long.'

'Good news for you, and for all Papists, then?'

Revill blinked – then gave a start as the other leaned forward suddenly.

'You see, I'm wondering what a Devon man is doing serving the Catholic League,' he snapped. 'Believe me, Perrot, you're not the first traitor I've been obliged to deal with over the years. So, I'd like the truth now – by the shortest route. I can't spare all afternoon.'

With an effort, Revill adopted what he hoped was a confident air, and drew a breath.

'My masters have long regarded you, Sir Edward,' he began. 'They know you have been a good friend, at times, to those of our faith. As they also know that you labour under certain disadvantages, shall we say, common to many in your position. It's never easy, is it, to manage an embassy in a city of this size? To entertain lavishly… to represent power, while the Privy Council are so parsimonious with money – as indeed, is the Queen herself.' He paused. 'Your pardon, sir, but you called for plain speaking.'

'I did,' Stafford replied; he was looking intently at Revill now, though his face bore no expression. 'You're saying I'm a pauper – is that it?'

'I'm told that you've been forced to accept loans from time to time,' Revill said, after a moment. 'Humiliating for you, perhaps… the Duc de Guise was one lender, I believe.'

The ambassador drew a slight breath, but made no reply.

'And so…' Revill forced a wry look, which he hoped would convince. 'My companion Auclair and myself are instructed – from the highest level - to offer you some assistance. Would you like a little time to consider that, before I go on?'

The other paused, then raised his cup abruptly and took a drink – a rather long drink, Revill thought. And when he watched him place it carefully on the table again, he was certain the ambassador's hand had shaken.

'You've come to offer me a bribe,' he said, very quietly.

Revill merely raised his brows.

'Well, then… pray tell me: how large a sum are we talking about?'

'A figure of ten thousand crowns was mentioned – at first,' Revill said, remembering Etienne's instructions from the morning. 'Yet that was deemed insufficient. We are authorised to offer you fifteen thousand, paid in tranches of three thousand at a time. Though that may be adjusted, if matters go well.'

'Adjusted, you say?' Stafford was breathing somewhat quickly, Revill thought. The amount of money offered was, as Etienne had said, enough to change his life utterly - to remove any troubles he might have at a stroke. It was a shock, which appeared to take him aback.

'And in return,' he continued, 'what is it that the good Duc might require of me?'

'I believe you already know the answer to that, sir,' Revill answered, maintaining a bland look. 'If I might speak plainly again, there are reports that you aided our friends in the past... provided small pieces of intelligence that were of value. Or perhaps, that you neglected to pass on certain tidings to the Queen's council in London, that would have been of value to them? For all of which, I should say, my masters are grateful – and they do not forget. Nor do they neglect to reward those who have taken risks... need I say more?'

'No, you do not.'

Stafford lowered his gaze and appeared to be weighing the matter. Finally, he looked up.

'So, assuming I did once pass on these... small pieces of intelligence, as you call them,' he said, with apparent calm, 'your masters would of course like to receive more. Concerning, for example, movement of the King's troops, details of despatches from England, and so forth – do I hit the mark?' And when Revill merely shrugged: 'For fifteen thousand crowns... a mighty generous sum. Could it be paid in French couronnes, perhaps, or gold écus?'

'I see no difficulty there, sir. Providing the-'

'And I take it that you'd like to have my answer at once – Englishman to Englishman, so to speak?'

Revill was about to answer that those were his orders, but he stiffened. A look had come over the man's face, which at first he failed to read – and then came the explosion.

'You whoreson Papist viper – get out!'

In a trice Stafford was on his feet, almost knocking over his chair. Revill blinked.

'By the Christ!' The man cried. 'I know I have enemies – as I know what the likes of Walsingham think of me! And I've made mistakes – what man hasn't? But whatever I've done, I've been loyal to my Queen and my country - I defy anyone to prove otherwise! Yet to think it's come to this… that I'm suspected of such base treachery… my God, I'm…'

He was almost speechless, flushed with shame and anger. In surprise, Revill too got to his feet. But he held his peace while the ambassador seized his cup, took a fortifying drink, then banged it down.

'Get yourself gone, Perrot,' he said, struggling to control himself. 'You blasted traitor… you, and all those snakes of Rome who'd sell their own countrymen! You're lucky I don't have you seized and thrown into the Bastille – but I won't. I want you and your whoreson friend to scuttle back to your *liguer* masters, and tell them they can stick their fifteen thousand crowns up their collective fundaments! And by God, when the King finally takes Paris – as he will, one day – I hope you and Auclair are among those hung from the walls in chains - you and Mayenne, and all the rest! Now go, before I draw blade and run you through myself!'

Without a word, Revill turned about and left him.

Though the room was not large, it seemed quite a distance to the door. Then he was out in the passage, where stood the servant who had ushered him in, wearing a look of alarm: clearly, he had heard the shouting. His mind racing, Revill faced him.

'I regret it was my part to deliver some grave tidings to Sir Edward,' he said quickly. 'The war stretches us all to our limits – and the messenger is often blamed, is he not? But no matter - with your leave I'll be gone. I have a long ride ahead.'

'Well, as you wish.' The other eyed him uncertainly. 'Your companion awaits you. He said he preferred to linger outside the entrance... do I need to conduct you?'

Revill shook his head: the servant was impatient to attend his master. With a dismissive gesture he strode off, reversing the direction of his arrival until he came to the main doors of the residence. There a different servant looked him over, before opening the doors – but as Revill began to step through, the man stayed him.

'One moment, please - aren't you forgetting something?'

Taut as a post, Revill turned... and let out a breath: the servant was pointing to his sword and poniard, which lay on a chest where he had left them. With a wry look, he took up the weapons and went outside. But as the doors closed behind him, he stopped in his tracks.

There was no sign of Etienne, anywhere.

***

With the afternoon waning, Revill left the ambassador's garden and walked up and down the Quai des Bernardins for a while, until he had satisfied himself that Etienne had truly gone. Whereupon, having no other recourse for the present, he made his way to the side-street from which the two of them had emerged barely an hour earlier. Thereafter, without much difficulty, he found his way back to the street where Elise Bodin lived, and paused outside the door. Just now, he had no notion what to expect; without his realising it, his hand strayed to his sword-hilt. Finally he lifted the latch and went inside – and froze.

Madame Bodin was seated at her table, holding a wad of linen to her face. Before her was a bowl of water, in which herbs had been strewn. As he entered the room, she looked up sharply, then let out a sigh.

'Madame?' Revill took a step forward. 'What's passed here?'

She gave no answer, merely lowered her eyes.

'Are you hurt?'

Still she said nothing... but with suspicions growing, he closed the door behind him and moved closer to the table. He had seen women in similar straits before, he thought – and when he caught sight of her eyes, red and puffy, he knew.

'Who did this?' He asked, feeling his anger rise. 'Was it Etienne?'

'*Arrêtez*... stop, please.'

She had lowered the linen pad, causing him to draw breath. A livid red mark covered half of one cheek, which would turn to an ugly bruise. Lost for words, he watched as she dipped the cloth in the water, wrung it out and placed it against her face again.

'It matters little,' she muttered. 'In truth, I did not expect to see you again.'

'Where is he?' Revill demanded. 'It can't have been long since he was here…'

'He left. He was angry – was it you who angered him?'

'If I did, I'm at a loss to know why,' he replied. 'But it's you I'm concerned for… what can I do to aid you?'

She met his eye, and seemed to relax a little. 'Some wine, perhaps.'

Revill went to the rear door, which led to a tiny kitchen and store-room. Finding cups and a flagon of the same wine he had already sampled, he moved back to the table and poured them both a drink. When he sat down facing her, she took a sip.

'He said you would not return,' she said. 'Why did you?'

'Etienne said so?' Revill drank too, then set the cup down. 'What else did he say?'

She gave a shrug. 'Nothing of import. I did not ask about his errand – your errand. He never speaks of his tasks.' And when he frowned slightly, she added: 'It is not how you think, between him and me. But there's nothing for you to do… you should leave soon.'

'I know that.' He looked down, trying to gather his thoughts. Surely, he reasoned, he had done all that was expected of him? He had carried out his mission: put the offer to Sir Edward Stafford, and received his reply. And if it was not the reply Etienne, and perhaps Baildon too had expected, what of it? The ambassador's loyalty had been tested – and in Revill's eyes, the man had responded admirably. Hence, what else was there for him to do now, but leave Paris at once and make his way to the Channel? Assuming that his horse was still in the stable where he had left it… the thought gave him sudden cause for concern. He glanced up, and saw that Madame Bodin was watching him.

'And yet,' she said, 'darkness falls soon, and the gates will be closed. Nor would I expect a man to undertake a journey on an empty stomach. You had best remain here one more night.'

'I thank you,' he said, after a moment. Then as the notion struck him: 'Do you expect him back? I mean Etienne.'

At that, her face clouded. 'Perhaps I do.'

'Then I would not leave, in any case. I want a few words with him first.'

'What, because of me?' She returned, somewhat sharply. '*Non* - I will not have *une bagarre* in my house. I told you last night-'

'There will be no brawl, madame,' Revill broke in. 'The man owes me an explanation, but I'll insist he and I talk elsewhere.' He paused, then: 'You have been kind, and I heartily dislike to see what was done here. In truth, I-'

'You wish to defend me, as last night when you thought a thief was come?' She let out a sigh, took the pad from her face and dropped it in the bowl. 'Well, Monsieur Perrot, then perhaps I should thank you.' She looked up. 'But that is not your true name, is it?'

After a pause, he shook his head. 'Yet it's the only one I may give you.'

She gave a nod, then added: 'And of course, he is not Etienne. But you will know that.'

Revill gave a shrug, and took another drink. Just then, he recalled Sir Edward Stafford telling him his wine was from Aquitaine, and that he detested the southern French...

'Is he from Limousin?' he asked, suppressing a yawn; on a sudden, he realised how weary he was. But at his question, Madame Bodin let out a short laugh.

'Him? No! Have you not guessed where he is from?'

He shook his head, whereupon she let out another sigh. 'Well, no matter... I am hungry now. Will you have cheese and bread, and sweet cake? It is all I have.'

'It will be a feast,' Revill said. But when she did not rise, he tensed slightly: she wore an expression he had not seen before.

'You're a good man, monsieur,' she said, after a moment. 'I thought otherwise when you first came.' Abruptly she stood up – and her next words stunned him.

'We will eat, and then retire. But I will admit this: I do not want to be alone this night. Your return was unforeseen... but perhaps it was timely.'

'Perhaps it was,' Revill answered.

'And so,' Elise Bodin continued, as if she had not heard, 'you will share my chamber - though I offer you nothing more than sleep.'

She threw him a faint smile, and went off to arrange their supper.

Sitting as still as a statue, Revill watched her go. His mind was in such a whirl that his only course, he decided, was to push the memory of this day behind him and let matters fall out as they would.

And so, he did.

SIX

Revill slept on the bare boards of the floor, wrapped in a coarse blanket under a quilted coverlet. Madame Bodin, for her part, undressed in the dark and climbed into the bed, which almost filled the small room. Thereafter, having wished each other a very formal good-night, they were still. After a while he believed he heard the woman snore slightly, though it could have been the wind: a breeze had got up, rattling the single window. Outside, the great city of Paris slept… but of course, he could not.

He had tried to order his thoughts, yet despite his relief that the encounter with Sir Edward Stafford was over, he was uneasy – and angry. He had been used, and then abandoned in a city loyal to the *liguers* where, as an Englishman who had fought for the protestant King, his life was in danger. He had to get out, yet was uncertain whether, if challenged, he would be able to give a convincing account of himself. Etienne, he had never trusted from the start… but why he had left the Quai des Bernardins and returned directly to Madame Bodin's was a mystery. And what of the man's anger, and his cruel treatment of her? Had he somehow guessed that the bribe offered to Stafford had failed? And if so, why should he be displeased?

Revill then thought of Baildon, which only increased his resentment. Having brought him here, the young man had simply disappeared; Revill should have looked in the stable already, he realised, to confirm that his horse was gone. He would do so first thing in the morning. Having resolved not to think beyond that for the present, he was trying to drift into sleep when a sound reached him, making him tense at once.

From the direction of the bed, came the sound of muffled weeping.

He remained still, uncertain as to his course of action: if he arose and tried to comfort her, would she misconstrue it, or be frightened - or might she even welcome it? He listened for a while, thinking that after some release of her feelings, she might fall silent. But she did not... and so, throwing caution aside, he sat up in the dark and spoke.

'Madame, can I aid you? Do you need anything?'

There was a sudden silence; he heard her sniff and let out a shaky sigh, then:

'*Mon dieu... peut-être j'ai besoin,*' she muttered, seemingly to herself. There followed a stir of bedclothes, from which Revill guessed that she too had sat up.

'Perhaps I do,' she said. 'And why should I not?'

After that, it seemed that she merely waited. And so, in the pitch-dark room, he got up from the floor and moved to the bedside. When he found the edge of the coverlet, he drew it back.

'Are you certain of this?' he asked.

'*Non* – I am not certain,' came the reply. 'Tomorrow you will be gone… yet just now, you may act as a man will.' But before he could comply, she added: 'First, tell me your Christian name – your true name - which I will use this night, and not thereafter.'

'It's William,' he said, after a moment. 'Most times, I'm called Will.'

'So… Will. I grow cold, and I would like to be warm. Does that please you?'

'More than I can say,' he answered. And putting aside all other thoughts, he climbed in beside her – then gave a shiver, as her hand came out of the dark to touch his face.

***

In the early dawn, with a faint light visible through the window, they lay side by side and began to talk.

For Revill it had been a shock: Elise's distant, even taciturn manner towards him throughout the past two days was gone, with a suddenness that took him by surprise. To his relief, once their unclothed bodies met she was passionate, using his name and urging him to do as he would. For his part, if he had harboured feelings of guilt that involved Jenna, they were cast aside by plain lust. He had been at war for months, with few comforts, and like any soldier who has survived combat he needed to assuage his desire. And thankfully, though she knew so little of him, she seemed to understand. So it fell out that, by the small hours, the two of them slept deeply, wrapped about each other. When he finally awoke, in some confusion, he turned to see her lying on one side, regarding him calmly enough.

'Your husband was a most fortunate man,' he said, after a while.

She gave a slight smile. 'What of you? Do you have a wife, in England?'

'There is someone,' he admitted, not wishing to say more.

'So I thought,' she replied. 'For you spoke her name, in the night.' And when he gave a start, she added: 'Katherine... is that she?'

'Ah, no.' In some relief, though tempered with sadness, he shook his head. 'Katherine is my sister... she has some trouble, back home. She's often in my thoughts.'

'She must be.' She put out her hand to touch him – and he would have done the same, until he saw her face more clearly in the dawn light, and the memory came back in a rush. A bruise was now visible: a blue-black stain, that made him start.

'By God,' he breathed. 'I burn to pay out Etienne for what he did to you.'

She paused. 'I believe you would, if I wished it. But you cannot stay.'

'No...' He gave a sigh. 'Apart from what I've found with you, I wish I'd never come here. I was forced to it...' He broke off, remembering that she did not want to hear what had brought him - whereupon she surprised him with an admission.

'I too am forced to act as I do,' she said. 'And it matters little if I speak of it, for you and I will not meet again.' And when he waited, she added: 'I am not the widow I claim to be. My husband is in England – in truth a prisoner, by order of Sir Francis Walsingham. He is the reason I must give lodging to the men who come here… men like you.'

He frowned - and at last began to understand. 'So, your husband is a hostage - how long since? Was it after you fled to England, following the… after Saint Bartholomew's?'

Now her face clouded; the memory of such a tragedy was painful. For a while she closed her eyes, then: 'It has been three years since I returned to Paris. They gave me money, and told me what I must do. So long as I obey, Antoine is safe… which is why-'

'By the Christ!' He broke in, as a notion flew up. 'Does my… does Castillon make report of you – hold power over you? I knew he'd been here before - that fey young popinjay! I thought there was something…'

'No, you mistake.' She put a hand over his mouth to stay him. Shaking her head, she seemed unwilling to say more, until:

'Not the one who goes as Castillon,' she said, removing her hand. 'He's but a messenger.'

'Well then, is there someone…?' He stopped himself. 'Etienne, of course.'

And to that, her silence was answer enough.

With a restless movement, he turned to lie on his back. Etienne, he realised, was Walsingham's man here, not Castillon… though how that came to be, he did not know. Yet it was clear enough what a hold the man had over Elise: the ease with which he came and went from her house, not to mention his brutal treatment of her. He faced her again.

'Which is why you don't wish me to avenge you,' he said. 'For it would go badly for you – and perhaps for your husband too. Etienne rules you – and uses you as he likes.'

She would not meet his gaze. But after a moment she reached under the coverlet, found his hand and held it tightly.

'Are you lovers, too?' he asked then, surprised at a sudden pang of jealousy on his part. He remembered vividly his and Etienne's first encounter, downstairs in the firelight – and found that his simmering anger at the man had just increased considerably.

'Enough… no more now,' Elise said, quite firmly. 'You torment yourself, when there's no cause. I'll rise now and prepare some food… then you must go.'

And with that, she sat up and turned away from him.

In the gloom he watched her get up, take a gown from a peg on the wall and pull it about her; then she was opening the door, still barefooted. As she went, she threw him a glance: one of the saddest looks, Revill believed, that he had ever seen.

But even as he arose to dress himself, he was forming a resolve: he was not done with Etienne yet.

***

Barely a half hour later, as Paris came noisily to life, he stood in a narrow street near the corner of the one where Elise Bodin lived, and waited.

Their farewell had been strained: he knew she was on edge at the likelihood of Etienne's return. After taking a hurried breakfast, standing up with sword already buckled on, Revill had paused by the open door, hefting his pack and his caliver. Emerging from the rear, Elise had pressed a linen bag into his hand, murmuring that it held bread and dried fruit. Then followed a brief but tight embrace, before she urged him to go. So, with a few muttered words of thanks – and of affection too - he had left her, stepping out into the street without looking back.

Once he had rounded the corner, however, he broke into a rapid pace towards the stable.

To his relief his horse was there, and appeared contented enough; Baildon's, as he expected, was gone. Using his limited French, he tipped the stableman a coin to feed his mount and ready him for a journey, saying that he would pay again on his return. Then, leaving his belongings, he made his way back to the turning, where he settled himself to wait.

It was a foolish notion, of course: he knew it, as he had a fair idea of the risks he was running, yet he had a compulsion to see this through. Already, he knew, he should be riding through the Porte St Honore and heading west – and yet, he stayed. He was outwardly calm, posing as an idler with nothing better to do, yet a deep resentment smouldered within him. Though it had shifted, since the early dawn - from mere anger at Baildon and at Etienne, to their master in London: not the dying Walsingham but his spymaster, and Revill's bane: Vice-Chamberlain Heneage, whom he had cursed on the battlefield by Falaise.

One day, he promised himself, he would find a way to free himself from the yoke Heneage had put about his neck – and more, the yoke he had likely put about the neck of Elise Bodin. He could not be certain, but the manner in which she had been forced to provide a haven for the Crown's agents in Paris, with her husband a hostage in England, had Heneage's stamp on it. Rightly or wrongly, the notion took hold: but just now, more than anything, Revill wished to punish Etienne for the way he had used her. And if he had to wait all day, so be it.

As matters fell out, however, that would not prove necessary.

Fortunately for Revill, since passers-by had begun to look somewhat suspiciously at him, only a short time passed before a tall figure he recognised at once appeared from around a corner, strode rapidly in his direction – and stopped dead in his tracks.

'You... *mon dieu*!'

'Surprised?' Revill enquired, stepping forward. 'Why? Did you think I'd fled, or was merely taken prisoner?'

Etienne frowned, but he was recovering rapidly. His hand moved towards his belt - but to his alarm Revill seized it firmly.

'No sense in attracting attention, is there?' He murmured. Meeting the man's eye, he jerked his head to the left. 'I saw a convenient ginnel over there. Will you accompany me?'

'Don't be a fool,' Etienne retorted. 'I'll call out, name you a thief, and you'll be seized.'

'But not before I've used this,' Revill said gently – at which the other jerked, feeling the point of a poniard pressed to his side.

'What in God's name do you want?' He demanded.

'You ought to know, well enough,' Revill answered. 'Now let's walk.'

Whereupon, to the other's discomfort, he placed an arm about his shoulder and, concealing the poniard with the crook of his elbow, steered him towards the entrance to the narrow side-alley. It was dark and noisome, smelling of urine, and deserted. After they had walked a few paces, Revill slammed Etienne's body against a wall and put the poniard to his neck.

'First, tell me why you left me at the ambassador's,' he snapped.

But his answer was a sigh of impatience. Despite his predicament, Etienne appeared unafraid... and he was growing angry.

'What need had I to stay? I knew you'd put the offer to him, hence-'

'But you couldn't know the outcome, could you?' Revill broke in. 'Unless, that is, you listened at the door?'

'For Christ's sake, stop this!' Etienne said harshly. 'I did my part, you did yours, and the task was finished. What need had you to delay – and why should you care what I did or didn't do? I thought you'd have got yourself horsed, and left Paris at once.'

'Well, I didn't,' Revill answered. 'I went to Elise Bodin's, and saw what you'd done to her.'

But if he had expected his reply to stir the man, he was wrong: instead, Etienne jerked his head back and broke into a harsh laugh. 'So that's the cause of all this,' he said, with a pained look. 'You, playing Sir Galahad?' He gave a snort. 'You bedded her too, did you? Well, lucky fellow - I hope to God you think she's worth it.'

Upon which, something happened that neither man had foreseen: in his anger and contempt, the one who went under the name Etienne had, for the very first time, allowed his accent to slip - and for Revill, the result was a revelation.

'By God – you're English!'

For a brief moment they eyed each other... until everything changed. With a speed that caught Revill off guard, his prisoner seized the wrist holding the poniard and bent it aside, forcing him to drop it while reaching swiftly for his own weapon. Instinctively, Revill's hand flew to his sword-hilt. Then he fell back and drew blade – just as the other drew his.

And so at last, they engaged: two enemies at bay… at which moment, as if the forces of nature had willed it, there came a pattering noise, and the rain began to fall in a torrent.

Yet it made no difference: his deep-lined face set in a scowl, Revill's opponent dropped into a crouch and spoke. 'You'll die here, my friend… on foreign soil,' he said quite coolly, in the accent of a Londoner, born and bred. 'You could have been far away by now, but you chose to meddle… a poor decision.'

'If you like,' was Revill's reply – whereupon, hearing the phrase that he himself used, the other man's anger only increased. He tensed, then lunged - but with an ease that surprised him, Revill parried it. Then he too lunged, forcing his opponent to parry even more quickly.

'A soldier… of course.' Etienne – for as yet, Revill knew him by no other name – gave a quick nod. 'Doubtless that little rat Baildon had orders to find one.' He tried a smile, but his teeth showed. 'It's no matter, Perrot – though I know that isn't your name. Perhaps you'll welcome a soldier's death.'

But Revill had ceased talking. His mind racing, he sought the means not to end the other man's life but to overpower him. He still wanted answers, and somehow he meant to get them. As the rain cascaded down, he side-stepped quickly in the slippery space and made a feint at the other's chest, but was prevented; for a tall man, his enemy's reactions were sharp. Their blades clashed – but Revill was doubly alert: Etienne still had a poniard at his belt, and could draw it at any moment. There was barely room for a classic rapier-and-dagger bout, yet he must be ready.

Whereupon, suddenly he decided - given the character of his opponent, and the narrowness of this stinking alley - to simply fight like an alley-cat. Catching the other unawares, he brought his free hand up, first and second fingers extended, and jabbed them hard into his eyes.

Etienne gave a yelp, his head flew back, and it was all Revill needed. Slashing at his opponent's sword-arm, he forced him to loosen his grip on the hilt. And in a moment, it was over: the weapon was wrenched from his hand and thrown aside, Revill had cracked him on the jaw with his bunched fist, and the man staggered. Scarcely aware of it, he found himself shoved to his knees, with a sword-point pressed hard to the cartilage of his throat.

'Now talk to me,' Revill panted, his fingers smarting from the blow he had dealt. 'Or I'll cut you piecemeal, until you spill your life's blood - here and now.'

In anger and helplessness, his eyes screwed up in pain, Etienne let out a gasp. As he did so, blood showed at his mouth – but at once Revill saw what he intended, darted forward and snatched the man's poniard from its sheath before he could move.

'That might be useful,' he said, breathing hard.

A moment passed, as his victim looked down at the livid red stain on his sleeve. 'You won't kill me,' he muttered, looking balefully up at him. 'You're the kind who believes in honour and mercy… an officer, I'd guess. You're surely no humble foot-soldier, who's been given a blade he barely knows how to use.'

'I don't need to kill you,' Revill said. 'I'll bleed you, as I said. Trust me, it hurts. You'll babble like they all do, in the end.'

Now, a look of unease passed over the other's features. Both of them soaking wet, dripping with rainwater, they eyed each other. Revill risked a glance round to the end of the ginnel, but there was no-one. Distant footfalls sounded, as people hurried from the rain.

'I knew the offer had failed, with Stafford,' Etienne said, with a sigh. He dropped his gaze, and a muttered curse fell from his lips: an English curse, familiar enough to his captor.

'Oh? How so?' Revill leaned forward, keeping his sword-point tight to the man's neck. 'You waited outside the door-'

'Until I heard the shouting,' the other snapped. 'That weak-kneed fool… trust him to dredge up some principles. As far as he knew, he could have become rich beyond his dreams-'

'But he refused,' Revill broke in. 'He showed spirit, and loyalty to his sovereign and to England – as he despised me, who played the traitor. And in truth, at that moment I despised myself! It was you and your whoreson masters who put me to it...'

His anger swelling as he spoke, he lifted the poniard and held it before Etienne's face. 'And yet, I still don't understand: Stafford was tried as you intended, and he passed the test. So, I'll ask you again: why did you leave so quickly, and go to Elise's? And what was the cause of your rage? Answer me, damn it, or I'll cut your ears off!'

'By Christ, to the devil with you!' The other cried, as if he no longer cared. 'Do as you will! I spoke the truth to you, the morning before we went to his house – that I believed he would grab the prize with both hands, and serve the League. Can't you guess why I was angry?' And when Revill merely stared, he let out a bitter laugh.

'Because I wanted him to accept the offer, of course, and be condemned for it! Hence, they'd be vindicated, back in London... Walsingham would be proved right, and Burghley wrong, and-'

'And you'd have your reward.'

The words flew from Revill's mouth, as at last the truth dawned: the hidden nature of his distasteful mission, and the reason Etienne wished him to assist in it. Breathing hard, the rain falling about him, he gazed into the face of this Englishman who spoke French like a native... this intelligencer whom he had assumed served the Queen's council, yet in the end acted for his own gain above all else.

Just then, in mingled bitterness and anger, he might have slain the man where he knelt… but he wavered; Eteinne saw it, and began to speak.

'Wait, before you act,' he said quickly. 'For no blame will attach to you. You did as you were ordered – as did I. My name's John Garratt, from London - Aldersgate Ward. And I serve the Queen, as you do. You may judge me as you like – but think first. Will you do that, for one who cherishes Elise, more than you can know – who would lay down his life for her, as I did for her husband? I pray you, spare my life. Do you hear?'

Revill heard, plainly enough. In the pouring rain, his mind spinning, he gazed down at the man who had revealed himself as John Garratt, but had no words. Instead, he took his sword from the man's neck, dropped the poniard onto the cobbles which were now awash, and began to turn away…

At which moment, Garratt struck.

Blooded and seemingly cowed, but with his base instincts intact, the man bent swiftly, snatched up his poniard and lurched forward. And though, alerted by a sound, Revill swung round and managed to evade a killing blow, he was stabbed in the side, the blade glancing off a rib. He reeled, but managed to lift his sword - and this time, all hesitation was gone.

In a blur of pain, he saw Garratt struggling to his feet, poniard raised again - and thrust downwards, into his assailant's heart. After which he staggered back, feeling warm blood welling inside his coat, and watched the man die as he fell.

SEVEN

A short time later, puzzled by a series of feeble blows upon her door, Elise Bodin opened it - and let out a gasp. Her hand went to her mouth… which was how, Revill remembered, he had seen her that first morning, when he had startled her by stumbling downstairs.

Just then, it seemed an age ago.

'Your pardon,' he breathed, leaning against the doorpost. 'But there was nowhere else.'

She hesitated only briefly, then took his arm. Moving heavily, rainwater running from his clothing, he crossed the room and sank down on a stool. Elise hurried to close the door, turned – and saw his doublet, stained a deep red.

'Can you climb stairs?' She asked, after a pause. 'You need to lay down.'

Blearily, he met her gaze. 'I don't believe I can.'

'*Non*? Then wait, before I make a bed.' She went off, and reappeared with a cloth.

'You must hold this tight to the wound,' she instructed. 'But first, show me.'

His face taut with pain, he struggled to unbutton his doublet until she helped him. Once it was put aside, they pulled up his blood-soaked shirt to reveal the gash where

94

the poniard had pierced him. Worse, there was a brief, livid glimpse of bone, before Elise covered it with the wadded cloth. Taking his hand, she pressed it to the spot.

'There's a man I know - a surgeon, who will help,' she said, breathing fast. 'But you have lost much blood… you need to rest.'

Weakly, he nodded - then as if for the first time, noticed her bruised cheek and remembered.

'There's something I must tell you.'

'Not now,' she replied, shaking her head. 'You must be still. Perhaps I can bind you-'

'Listen, please,' he broke in. 'You need not fear…' He sought for the words. 'Etienne… he's not coming back.'

She paused, a frown appearing. 'Why do you say that?'

He hesitated, as the reality of the events in that foul-smelling alley, but a stone's throw away, struck him with some force. A few minutes earlier, he had slain an agent of the English Crown and left him lying in a pool of blood. Whatever might come of it – assuming he lived to tell anyone – he would have to face the consequences eventually. Though now, there was just one priority: survival, with a distant hope of escape.

'He won't come here again,' he said, looking her in the eye. 'Because-'

'Because he is dead?'

The words sprang from her lips, as her hand went up, almost as if she might ward off the news. Then it fell limply to her side.

'*Mère de dieu…*' She sighed deeply, and her gaze dropped. 'I knew it would come… that one day, someone would tell me this.' She looked up. 'I never thought it would be you.'

'There's more,' he went on, with a sudden desire to get it said. 'I killed him.' And before she could react: 'We fought, and he told me. He's… he was not the man you think. He was English, and his name was-'

'John Garratt,' she finished.

A moment passed. Lost for words, still striving to keep his wound staunched, Revill peered at her. His mind was beginning to wander… he should do as she said, he was thinking, and rest. Later, perhaps…

He realised she was addressing him, and forced himself to focus.

'*Assez*… enough talk now,' she said with an effort. 'I will make a place for you to lie, then I'll go to fetch my friend. And you will rest, and be silent.'

With that, she turned and went to the stairway. Dimly Revill heard her ascend, then her footfalls overhead as she gathered bedding. After that, he had to struggle to remain conscious as she came down and busied herself in fashioning a makeshift pallet. Soon after that, leaning on her shoulder, he was staggering towards it, and falling…

The last thing he saw was her face above him, taut with concern, as he sank into oblivion.

***

A RELUCTANT TRAITOR

He believed that two days passed, though he could not be certain. Mostly, what he would remember later was pain and delirium: jumbled thoughts, and dreams punctuated with harsh words. People shouted at him, as if from far away: Sir Edward Stafford was one, telling him to get out of his house. Guy Baildon was another, and there was Etienne, saying he was an Englishman from Aldersgate. Finally, there appeared a figure that made him cry out: Sir Thomas Heneage, wearing a grim smile - and telling him that, this time, he was finished.

He had woken up briefly at that, grunting with pain. Putting a hand to his side, he felt a thick, taut bandage which appeared to pass right around his body. Moreover, he was naked, and clean and dry after his soaking. *How did she manage that?* he wondered vaguely, before slipping back into a blessed sleep.

When he finally awoke, he was in near-darkness and the house was still.

For a while he lay on his back, not wanting to move. The fever had abated, though he felt weak and very thirsty, while a dull pain throbbed in his side. Slowly he turned his head, and thought he saw a shape close to the fire, where a few embers glowed. He gave a start: for a moment he almost believed it was Etienne, as he had first seen him that night. But of course, he recalled with a shock, Etienne was dead... and he wasn't even Etienne...

'Elise, is that you?' He called, at which the figure looked round, then rose from a sitting position and came towards him.

But it was not Elise. To his utter surprise, a different face loomed above him.

'Baildon… good God…'

'Yes - only I'm Castillon still,' Guy Baildon said, speaking low. 'Are you, er…'

'Am I in health?' Revill muttered, as his thoughts began to arrange themselves. 'Well, I've felt better - and to blazes with your Castillon. You're Baildon, and I'm Revill.'

The other wore a troubled look, but did not reply. Instead, he moved to the table and returned holding a mug. 'Drink this,' he said. 'She left it, for when you woke up.'

'Where is she?' Revill asked. He tried to sit up, but the result was a stab of pain.

'Here… let me help, or you'll spill it.'

Baildon dropped to one knee, then to Revill's unease, put a hand behind his head and lifted it. He was able to drink, gulping the cool liquid down before he even tasted it.

'That's cider,' he muttered.

'It is, with some herb mixed in,' Baildon replied. Removing his hand, he allowed Revill to lay his head down.

'Where's Elise?' He repeated.

'Gone to bed. She was up all of last night, and the best part of today too. She's spent.'

'And what of you?' Revill demanded, as his words sank in. 'When did you return – indeed, where in God's name have you been, after you scuttled off and left me?'

At that the other hesitated. Finally, with a sigh of weariness, he got lightly to his feet.

'There'll be time enough for questions,' he said. 'First, I have to move you. Surely you know you can't stay here?'

'Move me?' Revill frowned - whereupon realisation struck him, like a blow.

'By the Christ… the body.'

'Yes, the body! Had you forgotten it?'

On a sudden, Baildon sounded as Revill remembered him: the withering tone, back in Evreux, the impatience laced with sarcasm. 'Did you think no-one would notice a dead man lying in a ginnel, with the rain washing his blood out into the street?' He demanded. 'There's been a hue and cry for the murderer, ever since.'

Revill closed his eyes, and wished he could simply fall sleep again.

'I don't know why you and he fell to blows,' Baildon went on; in the faint light of dawn that showed at the window, he shook his head. 'But before Elise told me you'd confessed to killing him, I might have guessed it. Though for now, your luck holds. They think the corpse is that of a Frenchman. With a little more luck, you can stay in Paris until you're well enough to get away - and after that, you and I are done.'

'That's the best news I've had,' Revill said, his anger rising. 'In truth, I wish to God I'd never set eyes on you. You led me here, then disappeared, forced me to wait on Etienne – I mean Garratt,' he added. 'That blasted double-dealer, I-'

'For pity's sake, stop!'

In the gloom, Baildon's hand went up. Breathing heavily, Revill watched him turn abruptly, and take a few paces. At the same time, he heard a sound above his head and stiffened. The memory came at once: of he and Etienne-who-wasn't-Etienne squaring up to each other in this very room, and waking Elise. He expected her to appear on the stairs at any moment, candle held aloft, but she did not. A moment passed, before Baildon faced him again.

'There's no use thinking of Garratt now,' he said, in a calmer voice. 'Doubtless this will come as a surprise to you, but there will be no recriminations. I mean, from London...' he gave a sudden snort that was almost a laugh. 'I spoke of your luck, just now... but even you will find it hard to compass what I'm about to tell you. You must have a guardian spirit that follows you about.'

'What do you mean?' With an effort, Revill struggled to raise himself; and though the pain increased, he managed to rest upon an elbow. 'What is it you're about to tell me? Speak!'

At that, the other moved towards the table, fumbling at his clothing. He must have produced a tinder-box, since

Revill heard the scrape of flint and saw the spark… then a flame sprang up, and a candle was lit. Dropping the box, Baildon came back to him, bent down and placed the candle on the floor. Then he was reaching inside the sleeve of his doublet – as he had done a week before, when the two of them had stood by the encampment at Falaise…

And when he produced the paper, visible now in the dancing flame, Revill saw the same seal upon it - and groaned. For a second, he almost wished it was he who had been left to die instead of another.

'From him?' He said hoarsely. 'Surely it cannot be…'

But, as before, Baildon merely held out the message. He had clearly read its contents, for the seal was broken. And, as he had done last time, Revill took it from him and read.

This time, the paper bore very few words. The order from Sir Thomas Heneage was terse, and quite clear: Revill was ordered to kill the one who passed as a Frenchman using the name Etienne; his true name was Garratt. The commission was to be done swiftly and discreetly, whereupon Revill should return at once to London and confirm that it had been carried out.

In disbelief, he dropped the paper and looked up to meet the messenger's gaze.

'When did this arrive?'

'In fact, it came with the order I first showed you – to go to Paris with me, and put the ambassador to question,' Baildon answered, calmly enough. 'I was ordered not to open it until after you'd seen Stafford.'

Whereupon he lowered his gaze. And not only was Revill speechless: even Baildon, it seemed, was lost for words.

**

In the early evening, the three of them took a tense and hasty supper: Elise Bodin, Guy Baildon - and Revill, who with some help had managed to get himself to a stool and sit. Thereafter, wearing only breeches and hose loaned to him by Baildon and wrapped in a coverlet, he had managed to drink and eat a little food, before resting his arms on the table.

One thought… one terrible phrase, had been echoing in his mind from the moment he had read the grim instruction from the Vice-Chamberlain: *I am his instrument still: both assassin and traitor. His carnifex, and his proditor.*

Little was said throughout the meal: a pottage of vegetables, heated up from yesterday's dinner that Elise had shared with Baildon. There was cider to drink, but no wine. What was left of that, it transpired, had been drunk by the surgeon who came to tend Revill's wound. He himself had no memory of anyone else being in the house.

'He will say nothing about you,' Elise had told him earlier. 'He will say he came to treat me for a sickness to the stomach. You are most fortunate, he said, that your lung was not torn. You will recover, he said. I trust him… he's of my faith, and a friend.'

To which utterance, however, Baildon had shown scepticism. He was insistent, and remained so: Revill must

102

leave the house, this very night. Now, with dusk falling outside, he repeated himself.

'There's no other way. Your horse is still in the stable, with your pack… which, by the by, is how I knew you were still here. You've been seen - and since the murder, as they call it, the entire Faubourg is astir. It's only a matter of time before someone comes here.'

'I'm not sure I can ride,' Revill said. 'Where are you proposing we go? Is it far?'

'It's too far for you to walk. We have to get you horsed… the ostler will help. He's a poor man, who'll keep his mouth shut when I've paid him.'

After that, since the matter appeared to be settled, Revill was silent. He glanced at Elise, but she did not look at him; in fact, she had hardly met his eye since he emerged from his fever that morning. Quite how she felt about John Garratt's death, he was unsure; despite her fear of the man, had they been lovers as he suspected?

He looked round; Baildon was talking again. The man had hardly ceased to blather, Revill thought, for most of the day.

'Do you hear me? You need fresh attire,' he said briskly. 'I'll bring your pack when I fetch your horse. You must burn the soiled clothing as soon as we're gone.'

The last words were for Elise, who nodded. And since the meal was over, she rose and began to remove dishes. Soon she was in her kitchen, where she busied herself in silence. The cups remained, however, and Baildon raised his. When he lowered it again, he found Revill's gaze upon him.

'Where is it you're taking me?' He asked. 'Is that where you've been, since you left here?'

'There's another house our intelligencers use,' Baildon replied. 'You'll be safe there.'

'Is that where Garratt was, when he too disappeared?'

'For pity's sake, how do I know?' Came the retort. 'He was a law unto himself, that one.'

'So you say.' His arms on the table, Revill eyed him. 'In truth, I learned that for myself, after our visit to Stafford. I was played for a fool, but one who was supposed to get a result: the result that everyone, it seems, expected - especially Garratt. But instead, our ambassador proved to be a better man, to my mind, and hence the-'

'Good God, will you leave it be?'

Baildon slapped a hand on the table, cutting Revill short. 'You with your piety,' he muttered. 'Knowing what I did of Garratt, you're lucky to be alive after drawing blade against him. And more – let me employ a tired phrase, since it's most appropriate: in putting an end to him, you killed two birds with one stone, did you not? Saved your own life, and carried out Heneage's orders, in one single act. Dame Fortune surely smiles upon you. Some might call it second sight - or even witchery!'

To that Revill drew a breath, but had no reply. Baildon's words were so blatantly, so ironically and so improbably true, that there was no answer. He wondered how long

Heneage, or perhaps Walsingham, had suspected Garratt of treachery. But if so, why would they entrust him with the mission to test the loyalty of the Queen's ambassador? Come to that, why had they chosen Baildon as a go-between - a man whom Revill himself had never trusted? His mind went back to their first, private talk in Normandy, when he had decided there was something odd about him; now, facing him across Elise's table, the feeling returned. Taking up his own cup, he made an effort to sit upright.

'Well then, I'm in your hands,' he said, having no stomach for further discourse. 'Why don't you fetch my horse and my pack now, and let's leave this place.'

'Gladly,' Baildon said.

And yet he remained seated, while from the rear of the house came the clatter of dishes. It struck Revill then that Elise might simply wish him gone – indeed, might wish that he had never come here at all. Did she intend to stay out of sight until he left, despite the closeness they had known - and despite all she had done for him, since his return? She might well have saved his life; the notion struck him, and stayed.

'And yet... there's one thing more.' Baildon met his eye, looking uncomfortable. 'It seems Garratt received news, with his last despatch - something I wasn't supposed to see. But since he's dead, I've been through his papers... it's a matter of delicacy. Of course, neither you or I would be allowed to learn of it. But the matter is...'

He trailed off, his face grave. Puzzled, Revill waited.

'The prisoner, Antoine Bodin… her husband,' Baildon went on, with a nod towards the rear. 'He's dead - in fact, he's been dead for months. She isn't to know of course, since, well-'

'Since she would no longer be of use to them?'

Revill almost spat the words out. But of course, he reasoned, as the import of the matter hit him, they would not tell her. It was plain enough: as long as Elise believed her husband alive – as long as she was caught in the vice Heneage had fashioned – she would continue to serve, providing a safe house for the Crown's agents. With Antoine Bodin gone, the compulsion was gone too… he breathed out, his anger rising. Was there no end to their lies - to their cold brutality? He would have said more, until he met Baildon's gaze, and frowned. Was he mistaken, or did the other wear a look of remorse – even of shame?

'Why, you dislike it as I do,' he said. 'You might even deplore it… the way she's been used. Can that be so?'

Baildon hesitated, his eyes still fixed on the table. Finally, he looked up.

'She deserves better,' he murmured.

'God's heart, she does,' Revill said. 'And so, will you take it upon yourself to tell her?'

The other made no reply, but lowered his eyes again.

'No?' Revill struggled to keep his voice low. 'Are you a coward, then, after all? For I never thought so… not when

I saw you wrangle with the guards at the Porte. Nor even when I first saw you in the wood, when you played King Henri's envoy and quelled Dufort and his people - and nor do I want to believe it now,' he added, with a pained look. 'But tell me: are you so fearful of your masters finding out, that-'

He stopped himself, as realisation dawned... while Baildon, for his part, could not bring himself to meet his gaze.

'So: you think she should know, yet you dare not tell her,' Revill resumed, after a moment. 'Instead, you want me to do it.' And when the other still failed to answer: 'In which case, I will do so – and to the devil with your unease. I owe her that, at the least.'

With that he too fell silent. Indeed, there was nothing more to be said, for the facts were stark. In silence, he watched as Baildon got up from the table.

'I'll fetch the horses now, with our possessions,' he said quietly. 'I will take a half hour, and no longer. Use the time as you please - but be ready.'

And with that, he turned quickly and moved towards the door. His coat was beside it, lying across a stool, and was snatched up at once. Then the door was open, letting in a cold swirl of air, and he was gone.

At the sound of the door closing, Elise emerged from the kitchen. Somewhat stiffly, Revill turned to face her.

'We have a little time before he returns,' he said. 'Will you hear what I have to say?'

EIGHT

The journey across Paris, through windswept streets peopled with figures hurrying homewards in the cold night, seemed to take an age; in reality, it was less than an hour.

They rode slowly, muffled and hatted against the chill. Revill was stiff and in pain, but at least he attracted nobody's attention as they crossed the Seine to the Ile, then crossed it again on to the north bank. Following Baildon's lead, he saw they were heading for the north-western quarter of the city. They had barely spoken since the young man had returned to Elise's house with the horses and the stableman. He and Baildon had helped Revill climb into the saddle. Elise had retired indoors by then, and did not wait to see them leave.

Now, with time to reflect, he recalled their conversation in the short interlude while Baildon was at the stable. He would not forget it, any more than he would forget the woman who for days had given him succour and shelter... and a great deal more, too.

It had begun with him bidding her sit down to face him, then telling her frankly of her husband's death - which news, she took with surprising calm.

'In truth, I had begun to suspect it,' she said, her eyes on the table. 'Yet, while there was a slim chance that he was alive, what could I do but behave as they expected me to?' And when he merely nodded: 'I knew the kind of man Garratt was - yet I trusted him enough to think that he would tell me.' She looked up. 'I was wrong.'

'So was I,' Revill said. 'I thought him a loyal servant of my Queen, but it seems he served no-one but himself.'

She let out a sigh. 'It pains me to think how he and I once were, a year ago when he first came here. What freedoms I allowed him... and what cruelty I bore.'

'He owed you a great deal,' he said. 'As do I – more than I can ever repay.'

'Let us not speak of that now,' she said, with an effort. 'You at least, I believe, have not lied to me - unlike Baildon.' Her expression hardened. 'He's a straw in the wind, and goes where it sends him. You should not trust him.'

'I don't,' Revill told her.

For a moment it looked as if she would say more, but she held back. Thinking she wished to be alone he tried to rise, but with a gesture she stayed him.

'Before you leave here, let me speak,' she said. 'In truth, I don't regret what you and I did.' And when he met her gaze: 'You're a kindly man, for all your soldierly ways. And you have been forced to act - as I was - against your will. Yet I, perhaps, am free now. My hope is that you too may be able to break free of what shackles you, and find peace.'

He asked her what she would do, now that the news of her husband's death had been told.

'I will mourn, as best I can. Even though there's no body to bury.'

Whereupon at last, she seemed to be biting back tears. 'First, I'll go to pray,' she said finally. 'And then perhaps I will make plans to leave Paris, for there's nothing to keep me. Almost all of my family are gone... even those who survived Bartholomew fled, long ago.'

'You could go back to England, and live among your fellow Huguenots,' Revill said. 'There are many in London still.'

'I know...' She met his gaze - then to his relief put out a hand, which he clasped at once. 'But if I did, I would be unhappy. I would think of Antoine too much... he was a man of courage, as are you. Now, you must make ready to leave – and I pray you will be safe.'

With that, she had withdrawn her hand and got to her feet. Revill's last memory of her, after Baildon had returned with his pack and urged him to hurry, was of her standing by the doorway as they went out, putting a hand to her mouth as was her habit. Only this time, it seemed like a gesture of affection - as if she were sending a kiss.

Now, with an icy breeze swirling about him in the dark, he held the picture in his mind... and felt the loss of the woman who had saved his life. He came out of his reverie, to see that Baildon had drawn to a halt in front of him. Moving up alongside, he reined in and peered ahead. They had emerged from a street of what looked like closed-up shops into an open, triangular-shaped space lit by torches.

'This is *Le Pillory*,' Baildon said, turning in the saddle. 'You won't want to linger here.'

He gestured to an object in the centre: a heavy wooden post with a cross-beam, set upon a platform. A couple of beggars huddled at its base, swathed in rags and shivering.

'You can use it as a landmark,' Baildon went on, pointing to the left. 'That street takes you into the road northwards, which you follow to the gate in the inner wall. After passing through that you continue to the Porte St Denis, then you're out of the city.'

'That can't come too soon for me,' Revill muttered. He was freezing cold, the pain in his side had grown worse, and he was in no mood to be charitable. 'Can we get indoors?'

'We're almost there,' the other retorted. 'Just follow me.'

With that, he shook the rein and rode off down a narrow side-street, before turning into one even narrower. They halted outside a tiny, poorly-built dwelling, its windows shuttered.

'This is your safe house?' Revill said, frowning. 'I expected something-'

'Something grander?' Baildon broke in. 'You should be grateful to have somewhere to rest. I'll see you inside, then

I'll stable the horses. The keeper of the house knows me as Castillon. She hasn't a word of English – and moreover, she's almost deaf.'

Revill sighed and prepared to dismount – but the moment he tried, he was thwarted: stiff in every limb and in pain, he found it an ordeal merely to move.

Baildon saw his predicament and told him to wait. Getting down from his mount, he strode round to the house door and knocked, then opened it and went inside. He reappeared quite soon, followed by a squat, barrel-shaped figure barely four feet tall. Revill blinked.

'*Repliez-vous*!' Baildon shouted, gesturing in exaggerated fashion for her to bend down. '*Allez - vite*!'

To Revill's surprise, the strange little woman shuffled towards his horse and bent low beside his stirrup to form a footstool. Baildon came close, telling him to lift both feet free and swivel his body to their side, which he managed to do. And hence, with pain but without too much difficulty, he was able to lower his weight onto the servant's broad back, and at last put his feet to the ground. There he stood, breathing hard, while she straightened up with a groan.

'*Merci, madame*,' he murmured – then, when she ignored him, remembered.

'She hasn't heard,' Baildon said. 'Follow her in, and make signals as to what you need.'

With that, he moved off to take the reins of both horses. The dwarf, meanwhile, with a brief gesture in Revill's direction, waddled through the doorway. He followed her, finding himself in a cluttered room that looked like a workshop of some kind, lit by smoky lanterns. Then his host turned about, and for the first time he saw her face: pudgy and framed by grey hair - and with one eye covered. The covering, on a band round her head, was a patch of black cloth, neatly embroidered with an image of a white, staring eye with a blue iris.

'*Vous l'aimez?*' The woman said loudly, summoning a gap-toothed grin. Upon seeing his startled expression, she gave a shout of laughter.

Revill would have liked to reply: yes, he liked the device well enough. But he merely stared.

***

When he awoke the next morning, there was an eerie light in the room, which at first puzzled him. Slowly, the contours of the place became clear, with its clutter of furniture and what looked like piles of clothing; the shutters, he saw, were open. Meanwhile he grew aware of street sounds from outside: crisply defined, with a familiar kind of echo – and then he understood: there had been a snowfall in the night, and Paris would be carpeted in white.

There were other sounds too, from close by, which he failed to identify. Struggling to sit up, he found that he could do so; the soreness was still there, but diminished. He had slept well, on a tightly-stuffed, if none-too-clean straw pallet, and was relieved to feel a little stronger. He

113

glanced round, saw a little stone fireplace where a fire burned, and a crude stairway to the upper floor, like a Jacob's ladder set into one wall. Then he saw the loom: a rickety wooden structure that filled a corner, with heaps of coarse wool beside it.

As he stared, there came a rattle as the machine sprang to life, and at last he made out the diminutive figure of the dwarf woman, seated on a stool atop a pile of cushions with her back to him. She had not seen him rise but was bent over her work, peering at the shuttle. The treadle, he saw, had been raised so that her feet, clad in wooden clogs, could reach it.

So, she was a weaver. He was about to call out, then remembered that she was deaf; throwing the covers aside, he thought he would try to stand up. He leaned against the wall and put out a hand to support his weight, while easing his legs from under his body. With a heave, he pushed himself up – and breathed out in relief. He was on his feet, in some pain but steady enough. Surely it could not be long before he was able to take horse and get away?

Then there was noise overhead, followed by footfalls: someone else was astir, and it had to be Baildon. Revill retrieved his doublet from the floor, found his shoes and moved to a stool where he could steady himself to dress. The noise of the loom continued – then stopped abruptly. There came a muffled cry of alarm, followed by a stream of heavily-accented French, not one word of which he understood. Turning sharply, he saw the keeper of the house scramble down from her stool - to startle him once again, with the glaring image on her embroidered eye-patch. The two of them gazed at each other, until the other broke into a crooked smile, as she had done the previous night.

Revill mouthed an exaggerated *bonjour*, and nodded.

'*Ah - enfin!*' The woman cried, as a commotion sounded from nearby. Realising that her attention had shifted, he looked round to see Baildon descending the ladder nimbly. Turning to face them both, he gave no greeting but made signs to the hostess, who seemed to understand. With a last glance at Revill she shuffled away, through a low arch to a cluttered alcove beyond.

'Ursule will bring you food,' Baildon said shortly. 'I have to be elsewhere.'

Revill took in the news as he sat down to put on his shoes. Baildon was fully dressed, carrying his sword which he proceeded to buckle on.

'There's snow outside,' Revill told him, glancing up.

'I know,' came the quick reply.

'How long will you be away?'

'Why ask?' The other retorted. 'You'll want to be going soon, won't you?'

'You may wager on it,' Revill said, eyeing him without expression. 'But I had a mind to get some answers from you first. In truth, I've been feeling a little sorry for myself.'

'Then pray, accept my sympathies,' Baildon replied, without any sign of such. He was about to go, but Revill's next words stayed him.

'Aren't you forgetting something?' And when the young man turned with a frown: 'I'm to report to Heneage, assuming I can get back to London alive. He'll want assurance of Garratt's death, of course, but I could add a few other things. Do you see?'

'See what?' Baildon's frown deepened.

'That I might speak of you, of course.'

'Would you, indeed?' Came the frosty reply. 'Well, I hope you'll tell him how I saved you from fighting a duel, got you safely into Paris, aided you when you were close to death and then brought you to a private place to recover from your hurts. Will that do?'

'You might look at it a different way,' Revill replied. 'How you disappeared while I was asleep, and stayed away for days leaving me to wait for a man you named Etienne – knowing all along that he was an Englishman named Garratt. How you never accompanied us to the ambassador's house, though I was led to think you would. Moreover, how do I know you only opened the second despatch from Heneage when you claimed? You could have known already that Garratt was a varlet acting for his own reward - and hence to be snuffed out, as our Vice-Chamberlain might put it. It could have been me lying dead in that ginnel... and somehow, I don't think you'd have been sorry if it were. So, perhaps you'll see why I'm a mite ill-tempered today. Will that do?'

He raised his brows and waited. Baildon had stiffened, his bland expression replaced with a look of mingled displeasure and unease. For a moment he appeared to waver, then:

'There are things you don't know, Revill,' he said, with a sigh. 'Matters the Council entrust to very few men – and I assure you, I'm not often one of them. Garratt was, once… but in his arrogance, and being able to pass for a Frenchman, he thought to please himself. Heneage must have thought you were well-placed to remove the man. He's used you before for such tasks, has he not? And hence, he expected you to succeed.'

Revill said nothing, even though memories threatened to surface as they always did.

'And yet, we might talk later - if you're still here when I return,' Baildon added, turning away. 'Ursule will see to your needs. I suppose it's best you don't go outdoors. You'll attract attention – and a man who moves as clumsily as you do would be easy to detain, would he not? Especially in thick snow.'

Whereupon, catching up his coat from a peg by the door, he opened it and went out hurriedly, slamming it behind him. Revill sat motionless, taking in what had been said. Finally he managed to get to his feet, wondering whether he were fit enough to venture to the stable and check on his horse; surely it could not be far? He cared nothing for

Baildon's advice; he even harboured hopes that he might never see him again.

In that regard, however, he would be disappointed.

***

As Baildon had said, Ursule brought him breakfast: a thick, fatty sausage cut into slices and a pot of dark mustard in which to dip it. When he tried to ask for bread, she merely shrugged and left him to his own devices. Soon, and for most of the remainder of the day, she was working at her loom, weaving what he realised were rugs similar to the Turkish carpets seen in London, covering the tables of the wealthy. Then it dawned on him that Ursule's rugs were in fact designed to mimic those coverings: cheap copies, fashioned in a poor tenement in Paris rather than imported from distant Constantinople. Not that they looked cheap: he had to admire her workmanship, and the clever designs that had clearly been reproduced from the Turkish…

Suddenly, he thought of Jenna and her broidery skills, and a wave of homesickness came over him, quickly followed by a pang of guilt. Elise, of course, was still in his thoughts; while Jenna was in London, presumably lodging at the house of the haberdasher in Lombard Street. She knew nothing of what had happened to him, or even if he were still alive. Just then, he had never felt so far away from her – and from his gunners too, Tom Bright in particular. When he might see any of them again, he could not know. In truth, he thought ruefully, he might as well be watching rugs being woven in the land of the Great Turk… a barbarian? Someone had used that word to him not long ago, he recalled; but just now, he could not remember who.

And so, he spent the day as best he could: walking about to exercise himself, drinking plain water from a jug that sat on Ursule's small table, and eating the poor fare she brought him at mid-day: a hunk of deep-yellow cheese and a piece of pie, the contents of which he preferred not to speculate on. In the afternoon he removed his bandage, and was relieved to find that the wound was healing as the surgeon had foretold. Begging a strip of linen from Ursule – which she was loth to provide until he paid - he made up a fresh bandage and tied it tightly about himself. After that he settled down to rest, finally sleeping until dusk.

When he awoke, however, he was fretful: Baildon had not returned, and Revill himself doubted whether he was fit to ride far; he had not gone out to the stable after all. Another night loomed in this place, on the foul-smelling pallet, perhaps even another day too. Beyond that, all was uncertain… until in the early evening, after he had helped Ursule light the lanterns and stoke the fire, matters fell out differently.

The first he knew, while hoping for some supper, was the door opening, bringing in a blast of freezing-cold air. Seated at the table, Revill looked up quickly.

But it was not Baildon. It was a man he had not seen before: dark-complexioned and heavy-bearded, dressed in riding clothes and a woollen cap. He wore a sword, and had a wheel-lock pistol in his belt. He strode into the house, saw Revill and stopped.

'Jean Castillon?' He enquired. '*C'est vous?*'

Revill decided not to answer. But he guessed one thing: the man was not French. Moreover, he looked every inch a soldier. A silence fell – to be broken by a shout, as Ursule appeared from her alcove. Scuttling forward, she bellowed at the intruder, making gestures anyone could understand. With a muffled curse, the man turned and kicked the door shut.

'Castillon?' He repeated, taking a step towards the table.

Once again Revill refrained from answering, whereupon the other peered down at him with growing suspicion. But he was distracted by Ursule, who stepped closer and began to address him angrily in her coarse accent. Clearly not following a word, the newcomer raised both hands to calm her down, before turning back to Revill with a pained expression.

'Do you speak English?' Revill asked him, on impulse.

'I do,' the man replied, with obvious relief. 'Will you tell this… person that I mean no harm? For I have almost no French, and I cannot understand her.'

Revill was tense, but contrived to hide it. With a nod, he faced Ursule and explained that this was a friend of Castillon. He would speak with him, he added. To which the little woman muttered something, before stalking off. She began to busy herself, apparently sorting through rugs, but did not fool Revill: from the corner of her good eye, he knew she was watching the dark-complexioned man like a falcon.

But as he turned back to the new arrival, his mind was busy: he knew a Spanish accent when he heard it.

'I asked if you are Jean Castillon,' the Spaniard said. 'I was told I would find him here - are you not he?'

'If I were,' Revill replied, 'what would you want with me?'

At that, the other grew impatient. 'I have ridden a long way,' he said shortly, 'and I do not have time for wasting.' He paused, then with a frown added: 'You sound to me like you are English, as I know Castillon is. Yet you are of the true faith, or you would not be here – so speak. Prove you are he!'

'Very well: I'm Castillon,' Revill said. 'But I am English, and my true name is Baildon.'

It was a risk that, later, he would barely understand why he had taken. But he could hardly admit who he really was: this man was an enemy. And yet, there was something more: a sudden desire in him to know his business. His distrust for Baildon was such that new suspicions had arisen – and after what he had learned of Garratt, he found himself wondering who among the Crown intelligencers could really be trusted. He might even learn something of value, he thought, and perhaps bluff his way out of his new predicament… but first, he must convince. Whereupon, a notion occurred that would solve his difficulty: he

121

remembered the small crucifix that Garratt had bought him, when he had been obliged to pose as an envoy from the Duc de Mayenne. It was in his pocket; drawing it out, he showed it briefly to the Spaniard, then placed it on the table.

'Are you thirsty after your journey?' He asked. 'There's only water, but I could ask the servant to go out for wine.'

'Wine?' The other regarded him for a moment... and then, to Revill's relief, relaxed visibly. 'By the saints,' he murmured, 'I have not tasted wine in three days... nor proper food.' Showing sudden weariness, he caught up a stool and moved it to the table.

'You offer me succour, sir,' he said, sitting down heavily. 'For which I am grateful. Send the... that hobgoblin in skirts out for wine, by all means. And tell her to bring something to fill my stomach too - I care not what it is, so long as I can chew it!'

With that he let out a breath and pulled off his hat, revealing a thick mane of coal-black hair. From one ear hung a short chain of gold, from which a tiny cross was suspended.

Revill managed a smile, and turned to Ursule. At his request, she came to his side with a wary look, but listened when he spoke loudly into her ear. This was an important man, he told her, who had travelled far and needed food and wine. If she would venture out, find a shop that was open and purchase such, Revill would pay her a couronne. Had she understood?

Fortunately, Ursule understood perfectly - and at mention of the fee, she was willing enough. She was a woman born in abject poverty, he had decided, whose work would bring in only a meagre income. It no longer surprised him that, at some time in the past, she had been persuaded to provide a secret house for English intelligencers, who might pose as customers for her counterfeit Turkish rugs.

Within minutes, clad in a heavy cloak that would have trailed on the ground had she not put on a pair of high wooden pattens, his hostess went out into the cold night. And as the door closed, Revill felt a sensation that surprised him: one of respect for this courageous little woman who, in spite of everything, had won his affection.

Then he gathered himself, and turned to face the Spaniard who, it seemed, was now his guest.

NINE

His name was Juan Carnicero, and he was no ordinary soldier of Spain: he was a carrier of official despatches who had ridden all the way from Flanders - and what he told Revill, over a jug of strong wine and a basket of pastries, stunned him. But the first thing he learned was even more of a shock: believing him to be Baildon, Carnicero was entrusting him with vital information - to be passed on urgently to the Duc de Mayenne's forces.

In other words, Baildon was a traitor; and on a sudden Revill saw that he was truly alone, among enemies.

After that, he was hard pressed to maintain an air of calm. For just as alarming, as the two of them sat quietly at the table by candlelight, was the knowledge that at any moment Baildon could return – and what might happen then, he could not imagine. In the meantime, he allowed his guest to eat and drink heartily, eating only sparingly himself and drinking very little wine. Throughout the meal, between mouthfuls, Carnicero explained his mission - and the tidings he brought were little short of momentous.

Two thousand Spanish troops under the command of Philip, Count of Egmont, were at this moment on their way from Flanders to join the Duc de Mayenne's forces, and so confront the King's army to the west of Paris. A major battle was brewing - one which might even turn the tide in the war.

Nodding gravely, Revill refilled the other's cup and encouraged him to say more.

'The King's successes – such as at Alençon and Falaise - are a blow to our leaders,' Carnicero told him. 'Mayenne is regrouping but needs reinforcements, which Egmont will provide. Yet, the matter is, we're not certain if the last despatches have reached the Duc - or even exactly where he is encamped now. Perhaps you can tell me?'

Combing his memory for knowledge of the Count of Egmont, the renegade Dutchman who had thrown in his lot with Spain, Revill kept expression from his face. 'Well, in truth I'm not certain of that myself,' he said, after a pause. 'I've been stuck here in Paris, with some tedious pieces of business. But of course, I could try to find out...'

'I fear there's no time for that,' the other interrupted. 'I have orders to go no further than Paris, only to deliver my despatches and then return to Brussels. You must go and find Mayenne yourself.'

'Me?' Revill blurted.

'Yes, you,' came the reply. 'For who else is at hand?' And when Revill made no answer: 'You could find yourself treated like a hero, when the Duc receives the tidings. His men are discouraged, and many others are dead or wounded. With Egmont's force they can stem the Protestant advance, perhaps even trample Henri of

Navarre into the mud… helmet, snow-white plume and all! Would you not rejoice to see that?'

Forcing a smile, Revill took a sip from his cup. Warmed and fortified by food and wine, the Spaniard was growing expansive.

'There's another thing,' he resumed. 'From what I hear, if I were you I would not remain in Paris much longer. It seems English agents have been busy here. One of our friends was slain a few days ago, who used the name Etienne – but I expect you know that?'

Revill lowered his cup, and managed a nod.

'He was found in an alley, in the south of the city… though I don't know the details,' he replied. 'He was a hot-headed fellow. Perhaps his masters in London no longer trusted him, and ordered his removal themselves?'

'Perhaps,' Carnicero grunted. He had finished the pastries, and sitting back, yawned long and loud. 'By the holy mother, I'm weary,' he sighed. 'I need sleep… will you arrange it?'

'Certainly,' Revill said, and turned about to look for Ursule. For the past hour, in a turmoil with what he had learned, he had almost forgotten her. But she was sitting by the fire in a low chair, half-asleep. When he called out, she jumped in alarm.

'Where in the Lord's name did you find her?' The guest demanded, jerking his thumb towards her in distaste. 'I was told where the house was, but I expected better than this.'

Revill merely shrugged. He was about to try and rise from the table, but hesitated.

'Who told the... our leaders of Etienne's death?' He enquired, with a casual air.

'Why - didn't you?' Carnicero replied, his brow creasing in a frown.

Cursing his clumsiness, Revill nodded quickly. 'Well, naturally I reported it as soon as I heard. Yet I didn't know word had left France so speedily.'

The other eyed him, then to his relief appeared to dismiss the matter. 'We're at war, Castillon,' he said tiredly. 'News travels swiftly... as mine must,' he added, meeting his eye. 'You'll have to ride out at first light tomorrow, snow or not. I'll hand my letters over to you when I leave.' He patted his doublet. 'For now, they stay on my person – even while I sleep.'

'I understand,' Revill told him. Whereupon he did rise, slowly and with an effort not to show signs of pain. His discomfort, however, was obvious even to Carnicero.

'You are lame?' He enquired, his frown returning. 'Will that not slow you down?'

'It will not,' Revill answered, sounding as determined as he could. 'The matter is too important. My horse is sure-footed, and I know the roads. You may count on me.'

And with that, he went to Ursule, and requested by means of signs and shouted instructions that she should make ready a bed for their important guest.

To his immense relief, Baildon had not returned after all. And with what Revill now knew, the man's whereabouts – both today, and those days when he had been absent from Elise's house – were the cause not merely of suspicion, but of deep concern. From the very start of their acquaintance, he realised – from their first meeting back in the wood by Falaise – the man had posed convincingly as an agent of the Crown, on a mission from Sir Thomas Heneage. And all along, he had been one of those rare but deadly characters Revill had heard of, who played a double game: intelligencers who served not their Queen, but her enemies. Moreover, it appeared, John Garratt had been another! The reality of it, the profusion of such treachery, took his breath away. It was a maelstrom, and Revill was caught in its centre.

But then, he had never trusted either of them: the arrogant Garratt, or the handsome, curly-haired young messenger. The matter angered him so that, had Baildon walked in just then, he might have attacked him on the spot. Though such action, he told himself, could have consequences in view of the other one who was spending the night here – and who, as yet, believed that Revill was Baildon.

So in a sense, he thought wryly, he would be killing himself.

***

The household retired an hour later: he on his pallet on the floor, while Carnicero took the bed on the upper storey

128

that had been used by Baildon. Should that one return in the night, Revill believed he would be ready… though exactly how he would act, he had not decided. He lay in the semi-darkness, propped against the wall with cushions. Ursule, who had taken a dislike to the visitor from the start, dozed off by the fireside wrapped in a shawl. Her snores soon filled the room, which Revill found helpful enough: he could not afford to fall asleep.

And yet in the end he did sleep, since all had been quiet, and the likelihood of the double-dealing agent returning in the small hours diminished. Hence, the next thing he knew was the clatter of booted feet on the ladder, waking him with a jolt. He opened his eyes to see Juan Carnicero descending in something of a hurry, and looked about to see that dawn had already broken. There followed a different sort of clatter: that of Ursule opening the shutters.

'*La neige maudite*,' she grumbled, cursing the snow. Revill sat up, relieved to find that there was only a little pain now. Then he gave a start: Carnicero was standing over him, shoving his pistol into his belt. He was dressed for riding, and taut with impatience.

'You should have told her to waken me,' he said, with a nod towards Ursule. 'I must make haste – and so must you.'

At this the memory of the previous night came back in a rush, so that for a second Revill was thrown. But he nodded and got stiffly to his knees, then to his feet.

'You are certain you can ride well enough?' Carnicero was frowning at him. 'Mayenne could be at Rouen now – that's eighteen leagues, at the least.'

'I know that,' Revill answered, though he had only a vague idea how far away Rouen was. And of course, he had no intention of going there; he must bluff - quickly and convincingly.

'I'll make myself ready at once,' he said. 'But will you not eat a morsel, before you leave?'

'There's no time,' the other replied. He looked about the room, his gaze alighting on Ursule who was standing with her arms folded, seemingly awaiting his departure.

'Can you trust that little harpy?' He asked, with a sceptical look.

'I can and I do,' Revill told him. 'She's half-deaf and knows no English. Nothing you told me would have been understood by her.'

'Well then, I will take your word.' After a moment's hesitation, Carnicero drew closer and put a hand inside his coat. A small package appeared, wrapped in oiled linen to keep it dry.

'I need not impress upon you the importance of this reaching the Duc,' he said, as he handed it over. 'You heard enough last night… and you said I could count on you. I will hold you to that – as indeed will our masters when I make my report. But for now…'

He broke off, looking round. Following his gaze, Revill saw the small silver crucifix still on the table where he had left it. Carnicero went to take up the object, and brought it over.

'Now swear,' he said, holding it out.

For a second Revill hesitated, then saw that he had no choice. He knew it, as he knew that somehow a new and terrible duty had fallen upon him: not merely to make this man believe that he would carry the despatch to the enemy - but instead, to find a way to get word to the King's forces.

For, as Carnicero himself had said, who else was at hand?

With feigned reverence, Revill took the cross from him. He bent his head, murmured a few words of Latin the other could not hear, then kissed it.

'*Hic juro*,' he murmured. 'This I swear.'

And with that, standing upright, he placed the chain around his neck.

'So, now I can leave you,' the Spaniard said, with some relief. He glanced at Ursule, who scowled at him, then started towards the door. But as a thought struck him, he turned.

'I stabled my horse in a hovel down the street,' he said, 'for there was nowhere else nearby. I saw a few mounts there, and one that looked like an English warhorse. Is that yours?'

Revill swallowed. 'Indeed... I once posed as a messenger to the King's encampment at Falaise,' he explained. 'My own horse being lame, I bought that one from an English farrier, then got away as quickly as I could.'

Carnicero nodded… then quite casually, spoke words that shook him.

'I thought so. For I could not believe that the only other good horse there was yours: a fine Spanish jennet with a white forehead. I wish I could afford to own such an animal… but then the likes of you and I are but messengers, no? Lowly servants are we!'

And with that, the Spaniard grinned and stuck out a hand. Revill took it, and was clasped in a fierce grip before they parted. After that he watched the man stride to the door, pull it open and go out, closing it with a bang.

'*Enfin*!' Ursule cried, with a gesture of dismissal. She shuffled off, muttering.

But Revill was not listening. Carnicero's words rang in his head: *a fine Spanish jennet with a white forehead*. There was no doubt: it was Baildon's horse. So, wherever he had been for the past day and night, he had gone there on foot. Did that mean he was close by?

Whatever the case, one thing seemed certain: he would be back sooner or later – and he would find Revill waiting.

***

It was mid-day before Baildon returned, and almost at once things went badly.

To begin with the young man looked tired and ill-tempered, and when he entered and saw Revill sitting at the table his humour only worsened. After shutting the door, he shivered, then looked round for Ursule. But she was seated at her loom, picking threads from a half-finished rug, and had neither seen nor heard him.

'So, you're still here,' he murmured. 'The sun's up, and the snow's melting. I thought you might have seized your chance - or have you sat on your rump the whole time I've been gone?'

'Where were you, then?' Revill enquired, eyeing him. 'I'd like to know.'

'Why?' The other countered. 'It's naught to you. Your work's finished here, so-'

'I thought it was,' Revill broke in. 'Now, I'm no longer certain. Matters have moved on a little since you went off.'

'Indeed? How is that?'

'We had a visitor.'

Baildon paused, and a look of uncertainty appeared. 'What manner of visitor?'

At that moment Ursule looked round, saw him and dropped the rug. Before she could get to her feet, however, Baildon made a dismissive gesture, waving her away. Facing Revill again, he repeated his question.

'A most unexpected one,' Revill answered. 'In short, he'd ridden hard from Flanders with a despatch for the *liguers*... most secret, too. I'm sworn not to reveal its contents.'

'You're what?'

With a look of mingled puzzlement and anger, Baildon stepped forward. As he did so, he saw that Revill was wearing his sword… a moment passed, as they eyed each other.

'The man… a Spaniard by the way, did I not mention it?' Revill went on. 'He and I had an interesting talk over supper. He spent the night here… a shame you missed him.'

Now a longer moment passed. Baildon lowered his gaze, seemingly thinking hard. Revill glanced round briefly and saw Ursule watching them. 'I suggest we continue the conversation elsewhere,' he said, with an edge to his voice. 'You wouldn't want us to fall to blows here, would you?'

'Fall to blows?' Suddenly the other looked alarmed; he knew Revill's qualities as a fighting man well enough. 'What in heaven's name do you mean?'

'I mean I learned something from our visitor,' Revill replied. 'Not knowing what Jean Castillon looked like, he asked if I was him, and I said I was. Following which, our talk was most engaging… quite a revelation, in fact.'

Whereupon, having said what he thought was enough for the present, Revill sat back from the table and waited - but when the response came, it was unexpected.

'Oh, good God.' Wearing a pained expression, Baildon sagged as if his strength had drained into the floor. He looked round, took the same stool Carnicero had occupied the previous night and sat down heavily.

'You're a meddling sort of man, Revill,' he said. 'How did I manage to get saddled with you?' With a weary gesture, he took off his hat and dropped it on the table.

Revill frowned, but said nothing.

'This Spaniard. What did he want of you – I mean, of me?'

'He wanted you to carry his despatch to the Duc de Mayenne. He seemed to have little doubt that you would do it - as one loyal to the Catholic League, that is.'

Revill spoke with a trace of contempt. He watched Baildon carefully - but still, the other's reaction was not as expected. With a sigh, he pulled off his gloves and threw those down too.

'You put me in a position I heartily dislike,' he said finally. 'But if we're to continue to work together, I'd best lay a few things forth – in secrecy. And there's no need for us to converse elsewhere, as you suggest,' he added. 'I've no intention of fighting you – and as you well know, Ursule won't understand us.'

For the first time, doubt arose in Revill's mind: this was not the behaviour of a man whose treachery had just been laid bare - or was he simply trying to bluff? Still wary, he watched as Baildon turned and shouted for Ursule. When she looked round from her loom, he made signs for her to bring something to drink, then faced Revill again.

'Naturally enough, you now think me a traitor,' he said quietly. 'But I assure you I am not. If you'll hear me, I'll explain - as far as I'm able to. Beyond that, you'll have to trust me.'

'Just now, that might be difficult,' Revill told him.

'I realise that,' came the reply. 'But you have no choice – indeed, neither of us has.' He paused, then: 'What was he called, the Spaniard?'

Revill told him, but the name clearly meant nothing. Whereupon Baildon asked him about the despatch. What did it contain - and where was it?

'It's safe,' Revill replied. 'As to its contents, I'd prefer to let you speak before I reveal them. Call me overly cautious if you like – or even a meddling sort. It doesn't trouble me.'

At that Baildon sighed, then nodded. 'If it must be so, I'd be obliged if you asked fewer questions.' He gave a snort. 'I seem to recall saying something like that before, back at the inn in Evreux. You were suspicious of me even then, were you not?'

But at the sound of Ursule's footsteps he fell silent. With a sour look, the diminutive servant dumped a jug on the table: the same one Revill and Carnicero had shared. There was just enough wine left to fill the cups she brought: again, the ones from the previous evening. When Baildon offered to pour, Revill shook his head.

'You'd better wet your tongue and start talking,' he said, as Ursule left them. 'For the contents of Carnicero's despatch are urgent, and need to be acted on quickly.'

'Damn you,' the other said then, with some vehemence. He put the cup to his lips, drank deeply and put it down, wrinkling his nose in distaste. 'If that's so, I need to see it now!'

'When I'm ready,' Revill replied, with icy calm.

'Then listen well,' the other threw back. 'Your loyalty and your resolve may do you credit, but your conclusions are wrong. You're a soldier, and not moulded to be an intelligencer-'

'That's so,' Revill broke in. 'And by God, I rejoice to hear it.'

'I pray you - enough,' Baildon said in frustration. 'Hear this, then: that despite what you think, the one who sits before you has served Queen and Council faithfully since the age of eighteen years. A pretty youth who spoke good French, and hence could be of service here - but not to the ones who believed he was theirs.'

He paused, drank, then looked away. 'Instead, he was groomed for murkier tasks,' he went on. 'Work that took him to the court of the Medici, and hence to that of Catherine herself, the last King's mother – here in Paris. Here he was admired, even treasured – and at last, forced to the basest of deeds: worming secrets out of perfumed courtiers while they sweated and panted over him, and called him their dove and their delight… must I draw an image for you, in all its tawdriness?'

He broke off again, looking down as if the very memories shamed him – which, Revill realised, was indeed the case. Stunned to silence, he watched Baildon lift his cup again, somewhat shakily, then lower it impatiently.

'The process may sound simple to you,' he resumed, without lifting his gaze. 'But it takes time - and a great deal of lying. Yet for one who was a born player, it was not long before he became trusted. And hence, moving among Catholics and posing as one himself, he found himself taken aside one day and invited to undertake certain missions in the Great Cause - even as far as the Low Countries. There, he shed his Papist shell and mingled with the Dutch... even with his own countrymen. And though he was frightened, he stayed long enough to gather such intelligence as he had been told to gather, and returned to his masters to be rewarded – patted on the head, like a faithful hound. But the same intelligence, I should add, he then misreported: altered it to give a very different picture to those masters, while the truth passed in secret to London. As of course, was intended all along.'

At last, he raised his eyes. But Revill had heard enough to grasp the implication of Baildon's words... and he was humbled.

'My God,' he murmured. 'I thought-'

'I know,' the other said, cutting him short. 'You thought I played a double game. Well, now that you know otherwise, I should tell you that you too are now in a perilous position. In short, if Heneage knew what has just passed between us, he'd have you killed.'

'I imagine he would,' Revill said, after a moment.

After that the two of them were silent for a while. Baildon drank, and gave a shrug. 'So, we must trust each other,' he murmured. 'I'll read this despatch, if you'll be so kind, and-'

'Garratt,' Revill broke in, as the notion flew up. 'What was he to you?'

'Oh… him.' Baildon wore one of his pained looks 'But of course, I can hardly blame you for your suspicions.' He let out a sigh, then: 'Garratt was reckless and greedy, and in the end a tiresome burr that had to be removed. Who do you think reported him to Heneage?'

'You?' Revill frowned. 'But the order to kill him came to me. I thought-'

'Your pardon,' the other broke in. 'But even I have my limits. I can do many things, but I balk at executions. As you've said, you're the soldier – and, I might say, a most reluctant traitor.'

Their eyes met. Realisation swept over Revill - but his anger at being used was dulled by the knowledge of the risks the young intelligencer would have run, these past years. One who, through his apparent innocence, was able to deceive people on both sides of this bitter conflict, and play what was likely the most dangerous game of all: not merely that of a double-dealer, but a triple one… he shook his head, and found himself gazing at Baildon with a new respect. He had learned, when he lay in pain on the pallet at Elise's house, that Baildon had already read Heneage's terse instruction: but it had never occurred that the young man himself was responsible for bringing it about.

'So - the despatch,' Baildon said at last, breaking his thoughts. 'Can I read it now, or do you intend to delay matters further?'

With a nod Revill put his hand inside his doublet, as Carnicero had done early that morning, and drew out the package.

TEN

The day being too advanced now, they decided to leave the next morning. Revill would benefit from another night's rest for the sake of his wound, and Baildon would venture out to buy food and other necessities. In the meantime, they took a meagre dinner and discussed their plans, for it was obvious that they would go together. Revill did not know the roads, and given the speed Baildon proposed to make, he might even have to be left behind at some point. The notion irked him; not only did he feel duty-bound to reach the King's army, and those courageous English leaders like Sir John Burgh who had stayed in France to fight on: there was another reason, that he finally admitted to himself.

If an important battle were indeed brewing, as Carnicero had told him, then Captain Will Revill should play his part in it. He had been idle long enough.

That event, however, seemed some way off. For the rest of the day, after informing Ursule that they would be leaving on the morrow, Baildon kept busy. In the afternoon he went out to the market and bought foodstuffs that could be eaten on the journey: cured meats, cheese and dried fruit. Meanwhile Revill exercised himself and cleaned his sword and poniard diligently, encouraged by the prospect of departure. By evening, having inspected his wound again and rebandaged it, he felt ready.

After an early supper, Baildon told him he must leave him again for a while, to seek information. 'You wonder where I go, when I'm away,' he said. 'Yet in view of what you now know, you'll understand that I have cause to meet with people to gather news… at times men of poor reputation, even some whom I loathe. But I need fresh intelligence now. For in truth, although I have a fair idea where Mayenne is at present, I'm uncertain of the whereabouts of the King. Wherever he is, we must find him quickly – for the Count of Egmont's forces may be closer than we think.'

'Then, I hope those men of poor reputation will speak the truth,' Revill said. 'For if I were in your place, I'd suspect everyone.' He glanced at Ursule, who was sitting by the fireside. 'Even her,' he added.

'You've no need to,' Baildon said. 'Her deafness is as real as her poverty.'

With that he got briskly to his feet, donned his coat and went out. Revill sat for a while, musing on the turnabout of events, then decided that he had done enough thinking these past days. On a sudden he yearned to be in the saddle again, though he missed Malachi. But he could at least take a turn outdoors, he thought, and visit the stable where his army horse was kept. As he found his coat and made ready, Ursule looked up. Having made her understand that he needed some air, another thought struck him: that throughout all his time here, he had not smoked his pipe. Small wonder that he had grown irritable.

A short time later he was in the street, stepping through puddles of slush. He soon found the stable, a dilapidated building on the corner. He entered to the familiar smell of horses, his eyes adjusting to the dim light... then stopped.

His own mount was there, but Baildon's was gone.

For a moment he was aghast. The young man had said nothing about needing to ride... what could it mean? In consternation, he ran the events of the day through his mind, recalling every word of his talk with the one he now knew was an agent of the Crown, posing as a traitor – or so he believed. Now, doubts surfaced quickly: had Baildon merely been bluffing, skilled liar that he was – even by his own admission?

He stood in the gloom, while horses stamped and snorted in their stalls. Once again, a weight descended upon him. In the morning, before Baildon's return, he had believed it had fallen to him to carry the despatch – but now, that document was in Baildon's hands, which threw him into turmoil. Was the man a traitor, after all? Had he played Revill for a fool - and instead of going out to gather tidings concerning the King's whereabouts, done precisely the opposite: followed Carnicero's instruction and ridden straight to the Duc de Mayenne – and by night, too?

In fact, that seemed unlikely: how would he get through the gates? And yet, the impossibility of his own position was stark. Not only was he in poor condition for a long ride - he had no idea where to go. Even Baildon was uncertain of the location of Henri's army at present - or so he had claimed. Was that too, merely a lie?

Being distracted, he barely heard the footsteps approaching. He turned sharply to see the ageing stableman standing nearby, eyeing him with suspicion. Summoning his French, he explained the reason for his visit hurriedly, then moved to the door. His only recourse for the present, he realised, was to return to Ursule's. He must spend another night as planned, then in the morning decide what to do.

Emerging into the dark and deserted lane, he was about to retrace his steps when hoofbeats sounded from behind. Instinctively he whirled around, reaching for his sword - only to stop in surprise.

'Revill? What are you doing out here?'

With a clatter of hooves and a splash of melted snow, Baildon reined in before him, his horse blowing gouts of steam into the cold air. Speechless, Revill stared up at him.

'There was no time to walk half-way across the city,' the young man added, somewhat breathlessly. 'And it paid – I found my man, and got what I needed. Though in truth, the tidings are troubling.'

With that he dismounted briskly, took up the reins and turned his mount towards the stable door. Then, peering closer at Revill in the gloom, he frowned. 'Is anything wrong?'

144

'No... nothing,' Revill answered, gathering himself. 'I... I ventured out to see that my horse was in good fettle. I'll come inside with you, while you unsaddle.'

'Yes, do so,' the other replied. 'From what I've learned, you and I won't be retracing our ride to Evreux tomorrow after all. To use your own words, matters have moved on a little. We'll be travelling westward, but by a road further to the south: through Pontchartrain, to the town of Dreux.'

Revill raised his eyebrows. 'I don't know the place... is it important?'

'It is now,' Baildon told him. 'Dreux is held by the League - but it seems it's under siege, by the King himself! Henri has moved south and east – faster than anyone thought. I can only pray that Mayenne's forces aren't moving as fast. Now, shall we get out of the cold?'

Whereupon, in a state of what now appeared to be excitement and nothing more, he shoved the stable door wide and led his horse inside.

Revill breathed out a sigh, and followed.

***

By the time the gate of the Porte St Honore was opened early the following morning, a handful of people had already gathered to make their way out of the city. But none was as well-mounted - or indeed looked as impatient - as the two men who sat apart, hats pulled low in the breeze. Mercifully, it was no norther but a milder wind from the south. Sitting his horse, Revill realised he had almost lost count of the days spent at Ursule's, let alone

145

since he had first entered Paris. Could spring already be on its way? In London the weather would be vile… but this was France. On a sudden, a memory flew up: of Tom Bright, grumbling as he stood on the Legal Quays below London Bridge, asking whether it snowed in France. It was only months ago, but it seemed like years.

It snows, he murmured under his breath. *And I hope you're back safely in London now, in your own bed - alone or not.* He looked up, as with a loud creak the heavy gates opened. Within a minute the two of them were riding through, and the great city was behind them.

It was a journey of around thirty-five miles, Baildon had said. They could not stop except to water the horses, and must strive to reach Dreux by nightfall. He was more than impatient: he was nervous, and Revill saw it. After he pressed him to say more, the young man admitted that the country between here and the besieged town could be crawling with *liguers* – patrols, or even larger bodies of troops. If they were challenged, they would have to account for themselves, and most convincingly. As he had done the last time they travelled together, he suggested that Revill might pose as his servant – or even act dull-witted.

'I'll be damned if I'll do that,' Revill told him, smarting at the idea.

'Then you'll need to think – and fast,' Baildon replied, spurring his mount forward.

Throughout the morning, as they passed through farming country, Revill found ample time to think. His immediate thoughts were of Ursule, and the farewell he had taken of her at first light. Having grown used to her presence, and with gratitude for giving him safe harbour these past days, he wished to reward the ferocious little woman. Money changed hands, but somehow it seemed inadequate... until he thought of the rugs she wove, well-crafted and all but indistinguishable from the Turkish. The notion pleased her, he chose a piece, and again money was handed over. Now the rug was spread beneath his saddle: a strong and comfortable protection for his horse, on the long ride ahead.

His last sight of Ursule was her standing at her door wrapped in a shawl. He had a final glimpse of the eye-patch with its lurid design... then came a surprise: a broad, gap-toothed smile of what looked like real friendship, before she raised a hand to wave him off.

Now, as he settled into the familiar, reassuring motion of the horse's gait, his thoughts strayed elsewhere. It was a relief to put Paris behind: the stronghold of the League with its fierce opposition to the new King, and an ever-present source of danger. It sobered him to think of what had happened there: the tense sojourn with the man he had known as Etienne, and their visit to the ambassador who had proved himself no traitor after all. But what had followed after made his spirits sink: the fight to the death in the ginnel, he knew, would be ever on his conscience.

But now, he breathed deeply of the air of the Normandy fields, shook himself, and saw that Baildon had drawn some way ahead. He was still uneasy at the notion that, in his eagerness, the young man might outrun him, his horse being the swifter; somehow, he must keep up. As for enemy patrols: though the road was clear, he found himself scanning every hill and coppice they passed. There had been the occasional cart, a number of people on foot and a few horsemen, but otherwise all was peaceful - until sometime after mid-day, it wasn't.

Having covered a distance of perhaps fifteen miles on what was for the most part a very straight road, Revill was uncomfortable. His wound had begun to trouble him, and he had a notion to ask Baildon to walk the horses so that they could drink from the costrels of watered wine they carried. The young man was a dozen yards ahead now… glancing aside, Revill saw a small wood to their right, on a slope. Baildon had spied it too, and was peering at the trees.

Urging his mount to a faster pace, Revill was only a short way behind him when there came a loud shout, and a sudden thunder of hooves. His horse shied at once, forcing him to tighten rein. Then he saw the riders: three of them, emerging at a gallop through the trees. Revill barely had time to draw close to his companion before they were waylaid and forced to halt. Without preamble, the leader of the group levelled a pistol at Baildon's head, and grinned.

'*Bonjour, messieurs*!' He cried cheerfully. '*D'où venez-vous?*'

Uneasily, Baildon returned the greeting. But to the question of where they had come from, he gave no answer. Revill sat motionless, wondering if the cocked pistol was primed and loaded… for some reason, he suspected it was not.

'*J'ai demandè d'où vous venez,*' the man said, grin still firmly in place.

Baildon hesitated. All these men, Revill observed, were rough-bearded and poorly-clad. More significantly, they were poorly-mounted too, and apart from the one who was their obvious leader, armed only with swords… turning slightly, head lowered, he spoke.

'They're not soldiers, they're nothing more than priggers. They want our horses and our valuables.'

'Why does he ask where we're from?' Baildon muttered.

'He's sizing us up, wondering how wealthy we are – and whether we might put up a fight.' Revill paused, then: 'I'd say we've no choice in that, wouldn't you?'

'I suppose I would,' the young man breathed.

'*Assez – taisez-vous*!' The leader's grin had faded. In rapid French he issued instructions, gesturing to them both to dismount.

'If we get down, we're finished,' Revill said. He glanced along the road, but there was no help in sight. 'You'll have to distract them – play scared – then I'll deal with the pistoleer.'

149

'My God.' Baildon swallowed audibly. 'I'm not a fighting man... I thought you knew.'

But seeing all three brigands growing restless, he drew a breath and held up both hands. Rather shakily, he announced that they would comply. He and his friend wanted no trouble, and they would be grateful if the gentlemen showed mercy and spared their lives...

At which point, Revill spurred his mount directly at the leader, leaned from the saddle and swung his fist, knocking the man's pistol from his hand. As it fell there was a click and a spark, but nothing more; if the weapon had been charged, the powder was damp.

The result was a very brief, taut silence – followed by mayhem.

With a roar, the group's leader yanked his feet from the stirrups and launched himself bodily at Revill. Not having time to get clear, Revill was overpowered – the result being that both he and his startled horse toppled over in a heap, trapping his left leg beneath it. Worse, his sword was trapped too, in its scabbard... then the full weight of his assailant was on top of him, driving the breath from his lungs. Desperately, he fumbled for his poniard: battle was drawn.

But it was not truly a battle; it was a savage brawl. There were cries and curses, as the other two men dismounted rapidly and closed in on Baildon, who was still mounted. Revill believed he heard the scrape of steel as a sword was drawn – but after that, he was too busy to do other than fight for his life. He glimpsed a flash of metal, saw his opponent's poniard rise, and his hand flew up to grasp the man's wrist.

Panting, straining with all their strength, the two wrestled for control of the weapon. Pinned under the horse, Revill was badly hampered; the other man was strong - and when he saw his opponent try to reach his dagger, merely pressed a knee upon his free hand. Meanwhile the horse whinnied and thrashed, flying hooves threatening them both. Looming above Revill, the prigger tried a surprise move, falling back and bringing his knee up to deliver a crack to the head – whereupon, as things were looking desperate, Revill had a thought. It was a familiar trick, which any old soldier might have scorned – but it was worth a try.

'*Pas encore*!' He cried, turning his head to look over his assailant's shoulder. 'Not yet!'

By some miracle, it worked.

With an oath, the man span round to face the non-existent rescuer - and that split second was enough. Revill let go of his wrist, whipped his own dagger from the sheath and plunged it into his opponent's neck. Breathlessly he withdrew the blade, producing a stream of gore… and what followed seemed to take minutes.

Dropping his poniard, the man made a choking sound, his hand clutching his neck. Rivulets of blood streamed between his fingers. He fell aside clumsily, then staggered to his feet. Dimly aware of a scuffle nearby – and a worrying yell of pain – Revill nevertheless forced himself to keep his eye on his enemy: it would not be the first time he had seen a dying man make a last, futile attempt at combat.

But there was no danger: reeling, coughing and bleeding, the leader of the highwaymen stumbled, then sank to his knees at the side of the road. Whereupon, with a supreme effort, Revill heaved his right side off his flailing horse, allowing it to scramble to its feet. He managed to dodge a hoof… and then at last, as the animal sprang away, his leg was free. Struggling to his knees, hurting in half a dozen places, he took his eyes off his dying assailant long enough to look round… and blinked in disbelief.

One of the priggers was on the ground, jerking in some sort of seizure, blood everywhere. Nearby was Baildon, still horsed, swinging his sword as if it were a racquet of tennis. But he appeared unhurt: Revill saw the shine on the sword as it dripped red, then looked round for the third man. At first, to his alarm, he could not see him… but three riderless horses were not far off, milling about nervously. His own mount, frightened by its ordeal, had run some distance away, where it came to a halt and proceeded to buck and rear as if frenzied.

Getting stiffly to his feet, Revill was at last able to draw his sword. Poniard still in his left hand, he turned to face the one he had defeated… and saw him fold where he knelt, mumbling to himself. With a moan he fell back on the grass verge, sighed, and went limp.

But it wasn't over. There was a thud of feet from close by, a savage cry, and a yelp which could only have been uttered by Baildon. Swinging round, Revill started towards his companion – but at once his fine Spanish jennet reared in fright, throwing him from the saddle. And even as Baildon flew into the air, arms wide, Revill saw the last attacker: he had been concealed behind the horse, and now loomed up with sword raised.

For a second, Revill thought he was too late: lying winded, his sword lost, Baildon was as good as dead. More, Revill would have another battle to wage, weakened as he was. But he gave a blood-curdling yell that he hoped would distract the assailant, and lunged forward. At once the man swung round, their eyes met... and then Revill saw it: he was hurt, bleeding profusely from his shoulder. Baildon must have fought like a demon on horseback, he thought... then he was dropping into a fencer's crouch...

Whereupon quite suddenly, his fears melted away.

He was a swordsman, but clearly the other was not; he was a battle-hardened soldier, but the other was not – and he had a vital mission to fulfil, while the other was driven only by greed. With a feeling almost of exhilaration – that at last, after what felt like weeks of failure, here was something he could accomplish - Revill smiled. And when his red-faced and sweating opponent wavered, he made a simple side-stroke with his sword that made the other flinch.

The man lunged - and lost.

Revill parried the blow, forcing the weapon aside, and thrust his poniard into the other's chest. Letting go of the handle, he fell back long enough to watch him fall, before turning at last to Baildon. Only when he had stumbled over to his companion, who was lying flat on the ground, did it dawn on him: they had been waylaid by three armed rogues who were now dead or dying, while the two of them were alive.

'Are you hurt?' He panted. Dropping his sword, he knelt down stiffly at Baildon's side. He saw no blood, but...

'I took a blow,' Baildon said, turning his head. He was pale and shaking. 'In the neck... I... I'm having trouble respiring...'

'Breathe steadily,' Revill said, his gaze going to the other's throat. 'Slow and even... I'll loosen your clothing.'

'No – don't. I don't want that.'

In consternation, Revill's eyes flew back to meet Baildon's. Was he so scared, he wondered, after what he had just been through, that he was jabbering?

'I have to do it,' he said, managing to sound calm. 'Your gullet may be crushed-'

'You mustn't!' Baildon insisted. Feebly he raised a hand, as if to prevent him. 'I believe I'll recover soon... let me lie here...' But he was breathless, the words spilling out in gasps.

'I can't do that,' Revill told him. 'You're weak and labouring. I might have to pierce your windpipe, make a hole and find something to put into it. I've seen it done, so let me proceed.'

'Oh, God…' Baildon let out a rattling sigh - then at last, to Revill's relief, appeared to give up. He turned his head away, his breathing shallow and rapid. Working swiftly, Revill loosened his jerkin and pulled it roughly apart. The doublet beneath was close-buttoned, right up to the neck. Aware that time was short, he fumbled at the buttons. With difficulty he freed one, then another, frowning at the tight buttonholes… a third came undone, until finally he lost patience. Seizing the lapels, he wrenched the garment wide… and froze.

Directly under his gaze, a thick band of black linen was stretched, very tightly, across Baildon's body. It was more than a foot wide, extending from the upper chest downwards, and appeared to pass right around his torso. For a fleeting moment Revill was reminded of his own bandage, that had staunched his wound for the past few days; he was even on the point of asking Baildon why he had kept silent about it…

Until he understood.

'By the Christ,' he muttered. Sitting back on his haunches, he exhaled. At the same time, he realised that Baildon's breathing was growing easier… and the windpipe was bruised, but not crushed. And yet, what he now saw – with a sense of amazement that he had never noticed sooner – was the throat: smooth and flat, with no adam's apple.

The band was there to keep a pair of breasts flattened - and thus far, it had served. Revill's thoughts were in a tangle, but one at least rose clearly enough.

Whatever his companion's real name was, it surely wasn't Guy.

ELEVEN

Now, it all made sense: the oddness he had observed in the young messenger; the delicate face and slight build; the timbre of the voice, not to mention the habit of sleeping fully-clothed, and the way he – or rather she - always managed to look clean-shaven. But still it was a complete surprise which left Revill feeling foolish - and somehow, used once again.

And yet, despite everything, they had no choice but to hurry on. Though sore and wearied from the near-catastrophe they had survived, their mission remained: to reach the King in time to warn him of the approach of the Count of Egmont's force. Once Baildon was back on his feet, fully clothed and buttoned, they set to work removing the evidence of their handiwork. Together they dragged the bodies of the three brigands away from the road, along with their weapons, and covered them with grass. Though for good measure, Revill took the leader's pistol. The riderless horses were a difficulty: standing about nervously yet unwilling to leave the scene. Finally, by slapping their rumps and shouting, Revill managed to drive them away, along the road to Paris. Only then did he approach his own horse, which regarded him warily before he was able to draw close enough to stroke its neck, muttering softly. At last, the animal tossed its head and permitted him to mount. Mercifully, in all this time there had been no other travellers on the road: another minor miracle, he thought.

But now, after they were horsed and moving again, their troubles had only increased. They had lost time, and had not even reached Pontchartrain. Baildon, silent and shaken, had recovered enough from the blow to the throat, and though bruised, was unhurt. But Revill's wound had been torn in the fight. He had taken time to undo the bandage, staunch the blood by pressing a wad of linen to it, then with his companion's help cover it again, tighter than before. The piece of linen was provided by Baildon, from what now looked to Revill like an over-stuffed saddlebag; that too, he thought ruefully, was something he had failed to notice. Far worse, he discovered that his caliver was lost, presumably when his horse fell and then sprang away; all he had was an empty scabbard.

His powers of observation, he told himself sternly, had fallen sadly short of late.

For a while they rode side by side, easing the mounts to a canter; Revill feared that moving to a gallop would prove troublesome. Finally, having borne the silence long enough, he turned deliberately to his companion.

'So – what in heaven's name do I call you now?' He demanded. 'For your name's no more Guy Baildon than it's Jean Castillon. And I'll ask the same question I asked you before, the day we first met: who the blazes are you - madam?'

'I was christened Arabella.' The reply came unwillingly, in a tone of embarrassment. 'Though in France, I'm known to some as Arabelle.'

'And your last name?'

'Does that matter?' The young woman – Revill had considerable difficulty adjusting to that reality – gave a shrug. 'And whatever I said, would you believe me?'

'Well, that's a fair question. And in truth, I'm wondering where your loyalties really lie.' Grimly, Revill turned to eye the road ahead. 'I've wondered that since we first met.'

'You've no need to fret,' Mistress Arabella said. 'I shall report to the King, or to Marshal Biron, and relay the intelligence concerning Egmont. After that you can go home to England. You're no longer bound to serve Henri's cause.'

'Does the King know who you are?' Revill asked. 'In fact, now I think upon it, who in God's name does know?'

'It's best I say no more. We'll part, and likely never meet again. And yet...' for the first time, she turned to face him. 'You'll always be in my heart, Captain Revill. You've served loyally and bravely... you probably saved my life, back there.' Her expression softened, almost to a smile. 'I spoke truly, did I not, when I told you I wasn't a fighting man?'

Revill had no reply to that.

'And more,' she went on, 'Heneage should know the true measure of the one he sends on such assignments. If I ever get the chance, I will tell him so.'

'Will you indeed?' Revill met her eye. 'So, Heneage knows you are Arabella?'

The answer was a brief nod, before she turned to look ahead. The horses had slowed their gait while the two of them conversed. Urging hers to a faster pace, she obliged Revill to make haste to catch up.

'I've heard how the French use female spies,' he said. 'You spoke of Catherine de Medici-'

'*L'escadrille volante*,' his companion broke in. 'The flying squadron... we were her stable, and we had our work. What I told you back at Ursule's house was true. The difference between myself and the others was that, whatever I learned was passed only in part to my mistress, but wholly back to London.'

Revill fell silent. He recalled their conversation of the day before: the tasks this agent had been obliged to perform to gain intelligence. The description of those perfumed courtiers who sweated and panted – he had thought it spoke of pederasty. Now he saw it differently... and on a sudden, was struck with a new respect for her that came close to admiration.

'So... when Catherine de Medici died last year,' he asked, 'what became of her stable?'

'Chaff to the wind,' Arabella replied. 'Though as far as I'm aware, no-one else assumed male disguise and got attached to the army of Henri of Navarre as a messenger. That was Heneage's idea... do I need to say more?'

'You do not,' Revill said. As it had so often, an image rose starkly in his mind: of the Vice-Chamberlain in his finery, wearing a sardonic smile. That cold, clockwork mind, with its uncanny ability to seize an opportunity for espionage... once again, he cursed the spymaster to the very devil.

After that they rode on for a few miles, meeting just one horseman along the way. There had been no sign of *liguer* patrols, or of troops. But already the afternoon was drawing on, and worse, dark clouds began to threaten from the west: their direction of travel. When, a short time later, they reached the village of Pontchartrain and stopped to water the mounts, Revill stepped close to Arabella and spelled it out.

'We won't reach Dreux before dark - you know it as well as I. More, there's heavy rain coming. We'll have to seek shelter, feed and rest the horses and attend to ourselves. If we do that, we'll make better speed in the morning.'

She faced him, seemingly about to object, but after looking up at the sky she gave a nod. 'Yet I don't want to stay in this place. It's probably full of *liguers*... we'll attract suspicion.'

'We might,' Revill allowed. Glancing down at his coat, he saw a small blood-stain that had seeped through his bandage. He straightened up and looked round at the handful of villagers going about their business – several of whom had paused to stare at the newcomers. 'I say we ride on a mile or two further, look out for a barn or a byre - if there is one.'

'There will have to be,' Arabella said.

It was settled. As soon as the horses had drunk their fill, they led them at a slow walk through the village, looking as if they were in no hurry. But once clear of the last cottage they remounted and rode on, breaking into a canter. Revill looked behind once, but they were not followed. Ahead, the ominous black clouds drifted closer.

Yet there was no sign of a resting place. They passed through fields, with the occasional glimpse of a small farm, but no isolated buildings appeared. More alarmingly, at one point a horseman came galloping up from the rear and passed them in a tearing hurry. As he went by he shouted something that Revill failed to catch, before hurrying on.

'What did he say?' He asked.

'I'm not certain.' Arabella was frowning, watching the rider disappear into the distance. 'I thought I heard *siège*… something about the siege? A despatch-rider, perhaps.'

'But from whose side?'

They exchanged looks, as the same thought occurred: was news already on its way to the King – ahead of them? On a sudden, the notion of stopping for the night looked unwise, or even reckless. Even in the short time since Juan Carnicero had brought his message to Ursule's house, and passed it innocently to Revill, rumours could have spread about the arrival of a new force from Flanders. In fact, neither he nor Arabella had any idea how close Egmont's troops were... might they even have reached Mayenne by now?

But just as Revill was on the point of saying they had no choice but to ride on, there came a flash of lightning, which caused his horse to whinny in alarm. The flash was soon followed by thunder - and the next moment the heavens opened. Almost at once the two of them were drenched, their vision blurred. The horses slowed, while about them rain fell in torrents.

'We can't go back!' Arabella shouted through the downpour. 'We'll have to move on, find some trees, or-'

'I know!' Revill called. 'Stay close – keep to the road, or we'll end up in a ditch.'

Shaking the reins, they urged the mounts forward through the curtain of water. They could see but a short way ahead and to either side, and the prospect was dismal. After a mile or so, Revill found himself contemplating a soldier's solution: merely to dismount, lead his horse to firmer ground, cause it to fall over and lie against it, in the lee of the storm. But just then a dark, square shape appeared to the left, a short distance from the road. At once he drew rein, tapped Arabella on the arm and pointed.

'A hut, perhaps... whatever it is, it will have to serve.'

With a nod, she turned her horse and walked it up a shallow hillside with Revill following, both of them bending low in the saddle.

The tiny building, however, turned out to be little more than a ruin: a shepherd's hut, probably used as overnight shelter during lambing time. There were no sheep here now. The land about seemed desolate... for now, the war was not far away. Revill believed he could almost smell it.

But this was all there was, and they had to make do. Dismounting quickly, he stumbled through the entrance – there was no door – and looked about. The place was empty, weeds growing high from the earth floor... but to his relief, some of the roof appeared solid: poles laid close together and covered with a thick layer of thatch. Rain dripped through in places, but one corner looked dry enough.

Emerging from the hut he found Arabella on foot, fumbling at her saddle-strap. 'I'll turn him loose,' she called. 'He doesn't mind rain... is there somewhere we can build a fire?'

'There is,' Revill answered.

After that they set to with a purpose, unburdening the horses and carrying all their possession in out of the deluge. While Arabella piled saddles, harness and packs against the wall, Revill hunted about for something to burn. Everything was soaked, so he decided to pull down some of the roof. Working urgently, his fingers cold and stiff, he broke poles into billets and made a pyramid on the driest area of the floor. Then he stuffed bits of thatch inside, stood up and spoke.

'There are cloths in your pack, and I need them. They're the only dry things we have.'

She did not hesitate, but went at once to the leather pouch and opened it. Revill took the pieces of linen, squatted down and pushed them into the pyramid. Finally he brought out his tinder-box, made a flame and touched it to the frayed ends of the cloths, then drew back in hope. The flame wavered, rose, then wavered again... but soon, smoke was curling from the damp wads of thatch. As it dried, there came a welcome crackle and splutter as the first of the billets steamed and blackened... then at last, it was alight.

He turned to Arabella, almost inclined to smile, and saw her gazing at him in approval. Together they watched the fire grow, knowing now that they could complete their journey.

Their shared, unspoken hope, however, was that they would be in time.

***

It was a cold night, and neither of them were able to sleep well. It was also one of the strangest Revill remembered: huddled beside a woman for warmth under the cover of his mock-Turkish rug – and feeling no physical urge whatsoever. Perhaps, he would think later, he had thought of his companion as male for so long, the habit had become fixed.

Mercifully the rain ceased soon after dark, and silence descended. They had eaten their food, sitting close to the fire while their outer clothes dried, draped on sticks driven into the ground. Revill sat in just his breeches and hose, Arabella similarly clad though with her chest binding firmly in place. She would not meet his eye, but nevertheless appeared to have relaxed in his company, particularly as he refrained from asking further questions. Instead he spoke of the morrow, and how their arrival at the besieged town of Dreux might be greeted.

'We must take great care,' he told her. 'I've known friendly soldiers be mistaken for the enemy when they ride up unannounced – even shot at by harquebusiers. Is there a convenient hill you know of with a vista, where we might stop and spy out the land?'

'I know not,' came the reply. 'For I've never been there. I suspect we'll have to shout, wave our arms and trust to luck.'

To that, Revill had thrown her a sceptical look and changed the topic. And a short time later they were lying back-to-back, as close to the fire as possible, while the silence outside lay heavy as a shroud. Once, after his companion had stopped fidgeting, he believed he heard distant noises; then he decided it was merely his imagination.

When dawn broke, they arose stiff and cold, dressed in silence and ate the last of the fruit. The fire had died out in the night, but at least their clothing was dry enough. Soon they were outside in a soft grey mist, packing hurriedly and saddling the horses. In the knowledge that they would at last be entering a field of war Revill missed his caliver, but there was no use dwelling on it. At least, to his relief, he was able to mount without too much difficulty. Then they were back on the road once more, making a good pace towards Dreux.

But after some hours, with a pale sun rising to lift the mist, an incident occurred which brought them to a halt – and changed the nature of their mission.

The way had been deserted with, once again, a disquieting lack of patrols or even messengers, from either side of the conflict. Indeed, the country seemed so peaceful that Revill was growing suspicious. He had drawn alongside Arabella and was about to voice his unease, when a sound from ahead put them both on the alert. Peering forward, they made out a cart drawn by a single horse, rumbling in their direction. There were no riders accompanying the vehicle, and only two people on the driver's bench.

'We might get news,' Arabella said. 'Dreux cannot be more than a few miles further.'

Sitting their mounts in the middle of the road, they waited for the cart to draw near. The driver was an old man, white-bearded and muffled against the chill, while beside him sat a boy, pale and shivering. With Revill and his companion blocking the road, the travellers had no choice but to bring the horse to a standstill, which clearly made then nervous. The boy stared at the two armed figures and gulped – whereupon Arabella, once again in character as Baildon, took charge. Easing her horse forward, she greeted both of them and spoke in rapid French, asking if they had come from Dreux – and if so, how had they escaped the siege?

Whereupon, with a start, she saw the people crammed together in the back of the cart. Revill saw them too: a woman and several children, swathed in blankets and trying to hide from sight. In a softer tone, Arabella asked pardon of the driver – but her answer was an angry retort which Revill did not understand. Thereafter, conversation flowed between the two of them, punctuated with gestures and a jerk of the thumb over the old man's shoulder, to indicate his passengers. Finally he stopped talking and waited.

'What does he say?' Revill demanded. 'Have they escaped, or what?'

'Not quite.' Arabella turned to face him. 'They've come from Dreux, and they're on the way to relatives… at a farm we passed yesterday, I think. But the news is…' she sighed. 'In truth, I'm at a loss whether to call it good or bad. It seems there is no siege – it was lifted two days ago. Henri's army has decamped to open country, to the west.'

'In God's name, why?' Revill found himself frowning, eyeing what he now saw were a family of frightened refugees. 'Why would he abandon the siege?'

Looking uncomfortable, Arabella turned to face her informant again and spoke further, receiving a brief reply. Finally the driver pointed at her and then at Revill, gesturing towards the roadside, and this time his meaning was clear enough.

'We must let them pass,' she said. 'They're poor folk, and there's little food left in the town. It's been hit by artillery...' she put on a wry look. 'Something you'll be familiar with.'

Revill stiffened, met her eye briefly, then looked away. Then, with a nod towards the old man, he shook the reins and walked his horse off the road. But Arabella remained where she was, fumbled in her clothing and brought out her purse. Leaning down, she handed coins over. Yet both the driver and the boy, who might have been a grandson, seemed either too wearied or too downcast to show gratitude. After mumbling a few words, the old man merely waited for Arabella to turn her mount aside, before he was shaking the rein and urging his horse forward. The cart rattled into life and drew away, the huddled figures in the rear now appearing like nothing more than a heap of rags.

'We'll likely be encountering more such people ahead,' she observed, as she drew up beside Revill. 'I don't like to think on what condition Dreux is in, or its townsfolk.'

'But that's not our concern.'

She looked round sharply, to see him eyeing her levelly.

'Henri wouldn't give up a siege without good reason,' he went on. 'He must have had news... what of the rider who flew past yesterday? Could he have been carrying word of Egmont's forces?' With an oath, he slapped the pommel of his saddle. 'Don't you see? We may be too late!'

He fell silent, glaring at Arabella as if it were somehow her fault; then, seeing her look of dismay, he let out a breath and relented.

'There's no use our going to Dreux,' he went on. 'Whether the enemy has already reached it, or is merely close, it's clearly a *liguer* town. All we can do is skirt it and ride on to where the King's army is. There'll be no difficulty picking up the trail of a few thousand tramping pikemen, not to mention horses and baggage train.'

'And if - when we find him, what will we report?'

She looked so dejected now that Revill had to pity her. He understood well enough: the haste, the desperate journey to carry the Spanish despatcher's warning - even, perhaps, the hope of some thanks for their efforts, if not a reward... had it all been for nothing? A battle could indeed be brewing – but in the end, what contribution could the two of them make? A wounded artillery captain without a gun crew, and a woman who was, by her own admission, not a fighter...

With a shake of his head, he slumped in the saddle. His horse, meanwhile, taking the hiatus as a time for refreshment, lowered its head and began cropping grass. Revill let it eat, his gaze wandering to the empty land about them, and finally back to Arabella. Then, quite suddenly, laughter bubbled up from somewhere inside him, and broke forth into a shout.

'By the Christ,' he spluttered. 'What a pair of dunces…
I wonder why we don't both throw the whole game up and
ride to the coast, take ship to Dover! You said there's
nothing to keep me here – but what of you? Do you think
the King will offer thanks, whatever pains you've been put
to? I say to blazes with Henri and his war – what say you?'

For a while they gazed at each other, until at last
Arabella's gloom seemed to lift. But she shook her head.

'Of course, you can leave – and you should,' she said
with a shrug. 'Willoughby's army will be home safely by
now – and besides, you must report to Heneage. If it's any
use, I'll pen a letter praising you to the heavens, saying
you've served admirably… or at least,' she added, 'I
would if I had ink and paper. Will a verbal testimony
serve?'

'I somehow doubt it,' Revill answered, after a moment.
'And from that, do I take it that you intend to ride on to the
King - with me or without me?'

To which question, her silence was answer enough. He
looked away, glancing idly down at his horse calmly
munching grass.

'Well then…' With a sigh, he raised his eyes to meet
hers. 'We can't have you blundering into a field of battle
alone, can we?'

He tugged the rein, forcing the horse to lift its head, and
walked it back on to the road. Soon he was urging it to a
trot, then a gentle canter.

Arabella followed, drawing her fine Spanish jennet to match his speed, both of them staring ahead.

TWELVE

The old town of Dreux lay peacefully under the weak afternoon sunlight. Smoke rose from chimneys, and there seemed to be no sign that troops had ever laid siege. Until, riding by the south of the town, Revill and Arabella drew closer and saw the evidence, the debris left behind by a withdrawing army: fields trampled into mud, a few broken carts, abandoned tents and assorted refuse... and a dreadful stink of open latrines, carried by the breeze that had sprung up. Drawing to a halt, they sat their mounts and gazed at the dismal sight.

'This poor, blood-soaked country,' Arabella murmured. 'Will it ever find peace?'

But Revill was in no mood to linger; to him, the aftermath of conflict was familiar enough. He shook the reins and moved forward, keeping the town's ancient walls to his right. And soon the two of them came upon the trail of the King's force, perhaps thirty yards wide: the earth churned by men and horses and rutted by cartwheels. It stretched away into the distance, towards open country. The land was dotted with figures: townspeople poking around, likely scavenging for whatever the departing soldiers might have left. Turning to Arabella, he suggested they accost one of them to see if they could learn anything.

173

With a nod, she indicated the nearest: a man in wide-brimmed hat and peasant clothing, who had spied them already. As they drew near, he tensed, gripping what turned out to be a hoe. Arabella at once assured him they meant no harm, but were merely scouting. He stood with feet planted firmly apart, eyeing them both suspiciously.

Yet the questioning was brief, for the facts were few and stark: the King had pulled back because the Duc de Mayenne's army was on its way to challenge him.

'How does he know that?' Revill demanded, once Arabella had translated.

But the answer came with a scornful laugh: everybody knows, the man retorted. Mayenne had already besieged Meulan, to the north-east - but since Henri had come to Dreux, the Duc had lifted that siege and was hastening towards him. He had a great army, people said: many thousands of foot soldiers and cavalry, led by noblemen and priests, along with mercenaries and Spaniards brought from Flanders…

On hearing which, Revill cursed aloud: Egmont's force had already joined with Mayenne - and hence, their mission had indeed been fruitless.

'I've heard enough,' he said in disgust. 'Shall we ride on?'

But the man was speaking again, growing animated and brandishing his hoe. Henri of Navarre was a Protestant pig, he announced, who would end up on a spit - roasted like a hog! When the forces of the League had triumphed a

Catholic would rightfully take the throne, and there would be no more foreigners roaming about France, sticking their noses in. Why, with God's gracious help the coming battle could be the last, he added... did the two gentlemen not pray for that, as he did?

'You'd best not tell him what it is I pray for,' Revill said dryly.

'There's more,' Arabella said, after another brief exchange. 'He thinks the King's army is heading for the Plain of St André... to the north-west, by the village of Ivry. If I know Henri, he'll make a stand there. He hates a retreat.'

'As it happens, so do I,' Revill said, turning his gaze upon their informant. Switching to French, he wished the man a wry *bon chance*, before turning his horse.

He would have liked to say more, but had no stomach for it.

***

It took only a few hours' further riding before the two of them reached the King's encampment, on the windswept plain between the villages of Nonancourt and Ivry. Long before they saw it – a great expanse of tents, horses and baggage carts, teeming with soldiers – they could smell it: the combined reek of horse-dung, unwashed men, old leather and rope. Yet on drawing closer, Revill was surprised at the size of the army: if anything, it had swelled since his last sight of it, back at Falaise. Banners fluttered, long picket-lines of horses stretched away – and then, he saw the cannons.

In surprise he halted, peering into the distance. He believed he could make out at least six pieces of artillery: culverins or demi-cannon, lined up on a low rise to the rear of the main camp. So, Henri too had received reinforcements; his gaze sweeping the area, he drew a breath. There had to be at least ten thousand troops gathered – perhaps twelve, or even more.

Arabella reined in beside him, seeming impatient. She had spoken of going straight to Marshal Biron, having assumed the persona of Guy Baildon again, and spinning a tale to account for her long absence. Beyond that, she had no plan apart from maintaining her guise as a loyal servant of the rightful King - something Revill found hard to understand.

'There will be a hellish fight here soon,' he said. 'You could be killed, or maimed and end up like one of those poor bastards you see limping about London streets, begging for charity. Do you think Heneage would grant you a pension? In your place, some might be inclined to confess all to the *liguers* and offer to serve them instead – if they don't hang you first.'

'What – do you truly think I could do such a thing?'

Angrily, Arabella turned on him. 'Or is this merely an embittered soldier talking? In truth, I think your heart has hardened by the hour, ever since we met that carter and his family…' she looked away, then spoke more calmly. 'Yet

I don't believe you're such a cynical man, Captain Revill. I think you'll fight for the King anyway, because our Queen promised to support him, and you're loyal. And because you have fought the Spanish, and you no more want to see a Catholic victory in France than I do, laying England open to invasion. There's my feeling on the matter – dismiss it if you will.'

'That's quite a speech,' Revill said, after a pause. 'Should I be chastened?'

She made no reply.

'Or should I even be flattered?' he went on. 'For in truth, I don't believe you're a cynic either - mistress. You may be an innocent maid, underneath all that swagger and scorn, but you have a strong heart. But now I suppose you and I had better part, and see if the King's commanders will give us something to do. You can carry despatches - and if you're wise, keep out of the fray. While I'll ride over to the artillery master, whoever he is, and offer my services. Is that how things stand?'

'I suppose it is,' was her reply.

And on a sudden, there seemed nothing more to say. Their sojourn together - of many weeks, as far as Revill could recall – was over. They had argued, ridden together and slept together, shared danger and disappointment, even assault - all of it, ultimately, in the service of Vice-Chamberlain Heneage, who cared for nothing save the success or otherwise of their assignments. For a while they regarded each other, before Arabella managed a faint smile.

'You asked me once, who knew that I was a woman,' she said. 'Ursule never guessed, and wouldn't have troubled herself in any case. But Elise suspected it.'

After a moment, Revill nodded. 'Perhaps that's why she never trusted you.'

'I know… and yet, she would never have betrayed me. And nor would you.' She met his eye. 'Which is why I ask this service of you: that you keep the knowledge of my sex a secret. I'm Baildon, and will remain so as long as I'm here.'

'But of course...' Revill smiled, then leaned from the saddle and stretched out his hand. 'I wish you well - Master Baildon. Just watch where you go, I beg… for my sake, if no other.'

Whereupon, without further word, they clasped hands and drew back, their horses stepping apart. Revill watched her ride off towards the King's banner, which drifted on the breeze among a cluster of large tents. Then he turned, shook the reins and began to make his way around the edge of the vast encampment, his eye on the distant slope where the cannons were mounted.

He could not know it yet, but it was to be an afternoon of surprises.

***

The first surprise, after he had been stopped by sentries and obliged to give an account of himself, was delivered

178

by the master of artillery: a hawk-nosed, moustachioed gentleman. As Revill led his horse into the gunners' encampment, the officer rose from a small table beside his tent, looking him up and down fiercely. Then abruptly, he broke into a smile.

'*Vous!*' He cried. '*Mais, vous êtes Revill, non?*'

Revill blinked, then gave a nod. 'I am indeed he, monsieur... do we know each other?' He spoke in English – and was relieved to hear the other reply in the same tongue.

'I saw you once, though we have not met,' the officer said. 'But I know what you and your gunners did at Falaise – destroyed the turret, and the marksman with it. We are men of the same calling, sir. I am La Guiche, master of the King's gunnery.'

They shook hands – but before Revill could speak further, the man floored him.

'So, you have come at last to take command of your men – excellent. I had no word of your arrival, but I am pleased. There are – how may I say it – some difficulties of language between my gunners and yours. Misunderstandings, unless I chance to be nearby to interpret.'

'My men, did you say?' Revill frowned. 'Surely not. My men returned home with Lord Willoughby's force, weeks ago. I have been occupied elsewhere... I came only to offer my assistance. If you have need of someone like me, that is?'

'But you are mistaken, Captain.' The other shook his head. 'Three English gunners are here, with the detachment of Sir John Burgh. They brought along their culverin…' he grinned again. 'Only Englishmen could give a gun such a name, eh? Fiery Moll!'

In astonishment Revill stared at him. An image flew up: of his last sight of the crew tramping off with the returning army towards Caen: Dan Newcome turning away from him gloomily… Tom Bright with head down, not looking back. Was it possible? He looked around at the handful of campaign tents – but La Guiche was speaking again.

'No doubt you would like refreshment, monsieur. Have you ridden far? I hope you will join me, for food and wine. We have matters to discuss.'

The artillery master gestured towards his field table, and a couple of stools. Trying to take in the news, Revill nodded absently… until his eye fell on a tent some yards away, with words daubed upon it. Sharply, he drew breath.

'I will be honoured to join you, Monsieur La Guiche,' he said, feeling his spirits rise. 'But will you allow me time to speak with my men? There are matters-'

'Of course.' The other nodded. 'Return when you are ready – the air grows colder, and we will sit inside.' He turned and called out in French, presumably for a servant.

Revill took up his horse's rein and led it away, his mind in turmoil. Three men, La Guiche had said, and one cannon: Fiery Moll. What of Spiky Bess, and the others?

Drawing near to the tent, he made out words painted crudely above the entrance in bad French:

Ici Anglais men. Non entrez sans boisson.

And yet the meaning was clear enough: *Englishmen here. No entry without drink.* Letting the reins fall, he stepped to the door-flap, lifted it and poked his head in - to be assailed by a fug of tobacco smoke. Wafting the cloud aside, he peered into the dim interior – and blinked.

With a look of amazement, Tom Bright sprang to his feet.

'Fuck me, Captain!' He cried. 'A miracle!'

***

There were three of them, it transpired, because the Kitto brothers had chosen to go on to Caen and return home. The others – Bright and Newcome, and the boy Lam Bowen - had other ideas. Or rather, they had been persuaded to change their plans and join Sir John Burgh's force in service of the King - and it was obvious who had done the persuading.

'The corporal couldn't bear to be parted from you, Captain,' Dan Newcome growled, seated on a box opposite him. 'Mayhap he felt guilty, after you fought a duel to save his neck.'

He eyed Tom Bright. No-one spoke - but there were grins on every face. Still giddy from the reunion with his crew, Revill sat on the beer keg vacated by his jubilant corporal and regarded each of them in turn: Lam Bowen, just as boyish but thinner in the face; Newcome, utterly familiar – and Bright, still draped in the fur-trimmed cape he had stolen.

'You're mad – all of you,' he said at last, with a shake of his head. 'You could have been home, safe and sound… haven't you had enough of this war?'

'I'd had enough of it before we even left Falaise,' Bright admitted. 'But you were staying, risking your neck… didn't seem right. Besides, Sir John's a brave man, about to go off to fight without gunners…' he shrugged. 'Well, it didn't seem right, is all.'

'The matter is, Captain, we were told you were with Burgh's force,' Newcome put in. 'Only when we caught up with them, you weren't to be found.'

'I got called away, on a foolish errand,' Revill said briskly. He caught Tom Bright's eye, silently bidding him to speak up.

'Well, it's done with,' Bright put in. 'Once we'd joined Sir John, there was no sense in turning tail again, was there? We should do our part – at least, that was my sentiment. Shame we had to say good-bye to Spiky Bess. The Kentish boys swore to see her safe on shipboard.'

'That's good to hear… and what of you, Bowen?' Relieved, Revill turned his eye on the youngest gunner. 'I thought you'd have stuck with your friend, Edward Kitto.'

Lam grinned uncertainly. 'The matter is, sir, I was tempted. But you and the corporal and Dan, you're like family now. I thought, if they're staying, well…' with a shrug, he broke off.

'So, you marched with the English contingent, on to Dreux?' Revill looked round.

'We did, Captain,' Newcome replied. 'Only there was nothing for us to do. We fired a few shots, then just camped outside the town...' he sniffed. 'I've never felt so stale. The place may have been full of *liguer* folk, but I never saw the sense in it, myself.'

A brief silence fell. Huddled round a little brazier of coals, with Newcome puffing on his pipe, the men raised their mugs: watered cider was all they had been able to get. After what had been said, however, a darker thought was in Revill's mind.

'You'll know – better than I, perhaps – why the King abandoned the siege and pulled back?'

Tom Bright nodded. 'We do: the enemy is on his way, and we must stop him.'

'That's about the size of it. And did you know Mayenne's been joined by a couple of thousand troops fresh from Flanders, under the traitor Egmont?'

'We heard rumours,' the corporal answered, with a sober look. 'If anything, that made it all the more worthwhile staying, given the way I feel about Spaniards...' he paused, then: 'Is that why you've turned up, Captain? For your timing was mighty good, was it not? Like I said – almost a miracle.'

'In truth, you might call it that,' Revill replied, after a moment. His mind went back briefly to the events of the past weeks, and the risks he had run: the terrible fight with

John Garratt, the altercation on the road with the three priggers. As if to remind him of how fortunate he had been, the wound in his side delivered a spasm, that made him stiffen.

'You're weary, Captain… you'll need to rest,' Bright said. 'Let me make you up a pallet. Though I doubt I'll be able to get you a tent to yourself, things being as they are.'

'Don't even try,' Revill said. 'After the way I've lived of late, sharing this bivouac with all of you will be a pleasure.'

He stood up, drained his tin mug and threw it to the corporal, who caught it with ease. 'Now I've got to talk with Master La Guiche,' he announced. 'Will there be a supper here?'

'There will,' Bright replied.

And from the look on his face, of relief that was close to delight, few would have suspected that he and the rest of them were about to face a battle.

***

As it happened, Revill did not share supper with his crew. Instead, as evening drew in, he sat in La Guiche's candlelit tent and dined at the officer's little table, waited on by his servant. The artillery commander was a genial host, and the beverage flowed freely: good Gascon wine, rather than the poor fare the troops consumed. After enjoying the first proper meal he had eaten in days, Revill sat back and voiced his thanks, which the other accepted

184

cordially. Soon, however, he was eager to talk of military matters.

'With your culverin, we are a battery of six cannon. Once the enemy is before us, on the signal we'll fire off as many volleys as can be done at speed, to cause dismay as well as destruction. Thereafter, the cavalry will charge – the King has three thousand horsemen.'

'Will that be enough?' Revill asked. 'From what I hear, Mayenne has closer to four thousand… they'll be ready to meet the charge, I'm certain.'

'That is true, of course.' La Guiche's thick moustache bristled. 'But they do not fight for a King, and his rightful cause. They are a mongrel horde – French, Spaniards, Germans, even Switzers, I hear. Once they feel the might of our brave army…' He broke off with a fierce look, and lifted his cup to drink.

But Revill gave a start: Swiss mercenaries? A picture arose: of Captain Werner, back at the Falaise camp, inviting him and his men to join with his company of turncoats and fight for gain. The memory shook him, more than he could have expected.

'Tell me more of your weaponry,' he said, changing the topic. 'Aside from Fiery Moll, you have five guns, you say?'

The other nodded. 'Five demi-cannon, with three men to each, and a goodly stock of stone *boulets*. There is no shortage of powder, which I have told your *caporal* I am pleased to share.' A grin appeared. 'He is a peppery little man, that one - is he not? Monsieur Bright?'

'He is,' Revill agreed. 'And I would trust him with my life – indeed, I would place the same trust in all of them. We'll serve you well – you have my word.'

Upon which he raised his cup and made a salute, to which the other responded. And soon afterwards, having agreed to talk again on the morrow, they gave each other good night.

Instead of retiring with his crew, however, Revill went at once to seek Sir John Burgh, the English commander. Word of his arrival might have begun to get around, he suspected – and the notion was reinforced when he found himself stopped outside Burgh's tent, under the light of torches fixed on posts. The one barring his way, a rather long-in-the-tooth, beetle-browed ensign, regarded him with a forbidding look… though beneath it, Revill believed, was unease. He began to state his business, but was cut short.

'I know who you are, Revill,' the officer said haughtily. 'Sir John is occupied just now, in conference with others. He'll send orders soon, though I already know what they say: that you and your gunners are to serve La Guiche, and be guided in all matters by him.'

'I understand that,' Revill replied. 'I merely wished to pay my compliments to Sir John, and make explanation for my absence-'

'Not necessary,' the other said at once. 'We expect to receive word of the enemy's position by morning; as you may have heard, he isn't far away now. Battle will be joined soon... are you not eager to play your part?'

'I am...' Revill found himself frowning at the other man's tone. 'Is there some reason you don't wish me to see Sir John? It's customary for a captain to pay attendance, surely?'

At that the ensign hesitated, dropping his gaze, before gathering himself to deliver the last – and most alarming – surprise of all.

'It's a delicate matter... one of honour, I might say. But you desire an explanation, so I will deliver it.' He paused again, then: 'There's a rumour among the French – among their chief commanders, I should say – that you are a coward, Revill. It goes back to Falaise, after the battle, when you were challenged to a duel by a captain of horse named Dufort. The duel, it's said, was cut short before it even began, by the timely arrival of a messenger who purported to come from King Henri himself. Moreover-'

'Wait - one moment.' Stung, Revill took a pace towards the other man, causing him to frown. 'I called for the duel to be suspended, because my opponent had the unfair and dishonourable advantage of a cuirass worn under his coat, hence-'

'Moreover - *sir*!' Growing flushed under the flickering torchlight, the ensign raised his voice. 'The very next day, this messenger and yourself left the army together –

187

without the King's leave, and not to be seen again! Hence, you may imagine that your reputation just now - as you arrive out of nowhere, after weeks of absence - hangs in the very balance… *sir*. Have I made myself clear?'

Revill stared at him, as the injustice of the accusation hit him like blow. After all he had done: being forced to embark on a detested mission, posing as a traitor, becoming entangled in espionage matters, not to mention coming close to death… he swallowed in dismay.

'Who else believes this?' He asked finally, his voice hoarse. 'Is it common currency among the men, or-'

'Fortunately for you, it is not,' came the terse reply. 'Lord Willoughby, before he departed, spoke for you, assuring the commanders that you must have had good reason for your actions. More, it was thought that word of this matter reaching the troops would be very poor for morale. So thereafter, the suspicions have been confined to just a few gentlemen-'

'Including Sir John Burgh,' Revill broke in.

His answer was the briefest of nods.

'And one or two highly trusted lackeys like you, perhaps,' he added. 'Privy to your commander's secrets – like how often he takes a shit?' Unable to keep bitterness from his voice, he stared the other man in the eye until he wavered. And yet, there was no point in further raillery; the ensign merely stood his ground and waited for him to leave.

'Well… then I will not trouble Sir John today,' Revill said heavily. 'But I tell you plainly that I did indeed have good reason for my departure – and that the duel, had it taken place, was rigged as I said. And let me assure you of another thing, my friend: I'm no coward, and if I must prove it by my actions in the coming battle, I will do so. As for Captain Dufort…' he drew a breath. 'If I get the opportunity, I'll drag him bodily before our leaders - or even a court martial – and have him give an honest account of the matter. But for now…'

Seething and sick at heart, he turned to go.

'For now, I wish you good-night,' he said. 'And *bon chance* in the coming battle – for both you and I, and every other man, will surely need it.'

Then he stepped out of the torchlight and strode towards his tent… to Tom Bright and the rest of his crew, who would never suspect him of anything even approaching cowardice.

THIRTEEN

Some days later, in the month of March, 1590, the great engagement took place over a single morning on the plain beside the River Eure, leaving thousands of men dead and many others fleeing in disarray. In the end, what would become known as the Battle of Ivry was a victory for King Henri the Fourth, even though it did not deliver Paris to him as quickly as he had hoped. But when the battle-lines were at last drawn, at dawn on that fateful day, no man could have predicted the outcome with any confidence at all – especially not Captain Will Revill. Standing on the rise with his corporal beside the row of cannon, he had a clear view across what was about to become a battlefield, and the sight subdued him.

There was no doubt at all: the King's forces were outnumbered by several thousand men. Moreover, the Duc de Mayenne had had time to assemble his impressive cavalry – many of them lancers, of whom the King had none.

'I fear this could go badly, Captain,' Tom Bright muttered, peering into the distance.

Revill looked aside to the gun crews. At the other end of the battery was La Guiche, in fierce conversation with his gunnery sergeant. The cannons' barrels were raised to high elevation, the trails wedged firmly, a pyramid of stone balls beside each one. The French crews milled about, talking among themselves. At this end of the line, meanwhile, Dan Newcome and Lam Bowen stood beside Fiery Moll, already charged with wadding, cartouche and ball. Newcome held the linstock, ready to light it from the small fire they had kindled nearby. The air was clear, with hardly a sound drifting from the distant array of enemy troops, save the occasional whinnying of horses. Beyond the ranks of cavalry, pikemen and others were massed in large numbers. Revill reached inside his coat, and felt the comforting handle of the pistol he had taken off a dead highwayman, back on the road from Paris.

And yet, he told himself, there should be no great reason for despondency. The King's army had seven cavalry squadrons, armed with swords and firearms, who would be effective at close range – who might even out-manoeuvre the *liguer* lancers, if they could evade their spear-points. And the commanders were men of valour, he knew, like Marshal Aumont, Count Givry and Baron Biron, the son of the Marshal. Moreover, there was, as La Guiche had said, the rallying presence of the King himself, commanding his own force of cavalry.

Soon after daybreak, Henri had made a rousing speech to the army. Sitting on his white charger, he had urged them to follow the snowy plume on his helmet. 'For if you will run the risk with me today, I will run the risk with you!' He had cried. 'I will be victorious, or die - God is with us!'

The cheer that followed was deafening – and doubtless audible to the enemy, men said, exchanging looks of encouragement. Among the small English contingent, however, the response was more muted. Dan Newcome merely spat and muttered that, as far as he knew, the Catholic League believed God was with them, too.

But now, a ripple of excitement was spreading through the King's troops gathered below: a stirring of horses, the clink of harness and stamping of hooves. Revill glanced at Tom Bright, who met his eye - then turned sharply to gaze ahead. A different sound had reached them, floating across the plain: a tremendous shout, from thousands of throats.

Mayenne was about to mount a charge – upon which, the artillery leaped into action.

Revill heard La Guiche cry out, saw him raise his hand, and snapped out the order to fire. There followed a brief flurry, as the linstocks flared and six gunners, Dan Newcombe among them, put fire to the little mounds of touching-powder. Splutters of flame sprang from the touch-holes, like a row of fireworks, followed at once by a furious roar as the guns spoke in unison. Below and in front of the battery, horses jerked and whinnied in fright, forcing their riders to control them, while clouds of white smoke billowed overhead.

For the artillerymen, however, there was now no time to do anything but work at speed, and be oblivious to all else.

The first volley, Revill believed, had little effect. At once, he went to the aid of his crew as they hurried to reload: Lam Bowen cleaning out Fiery Moll's barrel, Newcome bringing the powder-bag while Tom Bright seized a stone ball. Soon cartouche, projectile and wadding were being rammed home, while Revill took the linstock. Along the line the French crews were working just as feverishly, their shouts flying about the air - which on a sudden, had the scent of a battle that was about to erupt.

Revill smelled it, as did all the gunners: their faces set, wads of linen stuffed in their ears against the cannon-fire as they worked up a sweat. For some, younger men like Lam Bowen, there would be memories of their first battle; for others like Bright, Newcome and himself, echoes of more campaigns than they cared to remember. Bergen, Axel... his mouth tightened as the images flew up. Shoving them aside, at a shout of readiness from Bright he put fire to the touchhole.

The second volley rang out, as fierce as the first... and from the distance, a different sound now carried: like the hiss of pebbles on a windy shore – and a low moan, like the distant lowing of cattle. Revill stepped forward, shading his eyes, trying to view the enemy beyond the pall of smoke. From the other end of the battery came a cry: he whirled about to see La Guiche shouting in his direction. Putting a hand to his ear, he pulled out the plug of wadding and signalled that he hadn't understood...

Whereupon a third volley thundered out, sooner than he had expected, and deafened him.

His ears ringing, Revill staggered backwards. The French gunners, he realised, had got into their rhythm and shortened their reloading time by a considerable margin. But his own men were only a little behind... he had barely looked round before Fiery Moll roared again - bringing shouts of triumph from the French, and angry retorts from his own men.

'For God's sake, it isn't a contest!' He yelled. ''You'll overheat the barrel... Tom!' Stepping closer to his corporal, he seized his arm. 'Hold fire... bring water!'

But Bright was shouting something into his deaf ear. His head was ringing, as if to a tinkle of small bells ... he drew the plug from his other ear, turned and leaned close.

'We're done, Captain!' The corporal cried. 'La Guiche says to stop, or we'll be firing on our own men!'

For a moment Revill didn't understand... then he did. Aware of a distant rumble of hoofbeats mingled with cries and shouts, he whirled about - and swore loudly.

Mayenne had released the charge: a terrifying wall of horsemen, galloping across the plain towards the King's position, yelling in half a dozen languages. He saw a number of them levelling lances, and drew breath. Nearby the gunners, French and English, were turning to each other, voices raised in alarm... dropping ramrods and linstocks they crowded forward on the slope, gazing out at the fearful sight: four thousand *liguer* cavalry bent on routing Henri of Navarre's army, and turning it into a morass of mud and blood.

But that was not about to happen.

From below them came a shout, followed by others as the squadron commanders gave orders. These were followed by a host of answering voices, a jingle of thousands of sets of harness - and the King's horsemen rolled forward, away from the slope where the gunners watched, sweeping down across the plain. Behind them the infantry remained in place, pikes vertical like the bristles of a vast hedgehog, while the rear guard, led by Marshal Biron, waited their turn. His heart thudding, Revill gazed at the sight - and swore again.

Never, he thought, had he felt as useless as he did now: standing a safe distance away, out of the range of pistols or even calivers, watching a battle unfold before him as if it were a play upon the stage of a London theatre. Growing aware of someone behind him, he turned to face Tom Bright.

'Now he's truly embroiled,' he said, as Revill struggled to hear. Seeing his look of puzzlement, the sergeant pointed into the distance. 'I mean the King – do you see?'

Revill looked… and groaned. In a rush for glory, it appeared, King Henri was leading his own squadron forward, sword in hand and white plume bobbing. Behind him his men galloped furiously, their shouts clearly audible from the battery position. Meanwhile, Marshal Aumont was driving forward on the left flank, with the other cavalry leaders keeping pace on the other... until with a dreadful thud of colliding horses, screams of men and animals and the clash of weapons, the two forces met - and were plunged into chaos.

The mayhem lasted little more than a quarter of an hour; yet it was a bloodbath, as terrible as anything Revill had seen. Waves of cavalry broke and floundered, regrouped and charged again. From their hilltop the gun crews heard the din, eyed each other anxiously, then turned their eyes to the scene of battle, spreading outward like a massive stain. Already riderless horses were rearing and bodies littered the plain, while cavalry of both sides shot, hewed and hacked each other at close quarters... and now, came a repulse.

It was a squadron of Walloons, they would learn later, that turned the tide briefly in the League's favour, forcing a section of the King's horsemen back. French *liguers* followed, wreaking havoc among the milling riders. But quickly Aumont and Baron Biron countered, charging into Mayenne's cavalry. A cheer rose from the watching gunners as the *liguer* advance was checked – and another followed when they saw infantrymen running to join the fray: French royalists, flanked by English troops and others whom Revill at first failed to recognise... but when he did, he frowned.

'Switzers – those bastard mercenaries!' Tom Bright shouted. 'So, some of them are fighting for the King after all! They turn and turn like whirligigs!'

Revill stepped forward, beyond the line of guns, his eyes straining to see into the distance. He made out the King's snow-white plume, his squadron close about him as they clashed with the enemy. An oath flew from his mouth: Henri was racing headlong into the lancers.

'He's battle-crazy!' He exclaimed. 'He'll get cut to pieces…'

But he broke off as a renewed chorus of shouts and yells carried across from the field, along with more screams of wounded horses: Henri was among the lancers, seemingly unhurt and fighting bravely - and in a surprising turnabout, the enemy ranks broke. Despite their losses, the royalist forces had succeeded in getting close enough to render the spears useless.

And quite quickly, what some had feared was the unlikeliest of outcomes was changed to an exhilarating possibility - of royalist victory. One reason for it, however, no-one had foreseen: the abrupt surrender of a force of Dutch and German mercenaries on the *liguer* side. As men watched, both on the field of battle and off it, the entire squadron halted, fired their weapons into the air, then lowered their lances.

The result was a wave of shock that rippled through Mayenne's troops. Companies reeled and scattered, tried to regroup and parted again in confusion. And now many were fleeing… cheers broke out in pockets of the King's army, as the reality dawned. Already, *liguer* cavalry were turning their mounts away – and then, came the news that

197

would cause Revill's crew to raise their fists in the air for joy.

A despatch-rider on a sweating horse came flying from the field, back towards the royalist lines where the rear guard still waited. Drawing rein to speak hurriedly to the commander, the rider looked up briefly towards the gun battery. At once La Guiche hurried down the slope, calling out for news. The man rode quickly up to him, spoke, then galloped away – whereupon the French artillery master, wearing a grin, started back towards his gunners.

'What did he say?' Revill, ears still ringing, strode to meet him. 'Has the battle turned?'

'Joyous news!' La Guiche cried in jubilation. 'The Duke of Aumale has surrendered - and the Count of Egmont has been killed!'

Revill took in his words, let out a breath, and sat down heavily on the grass.

His mind was whirling. The mission... his and Arabella's race to warn the King of two thousand battle-hardened Spanish troops, on their way from Flanders... the grim realisation that the news was late, and ultimately useless... but now their commander was dead, leaving his men in disarray. In some way at least, it seemed to him, justice had been served.

He looked up as Tom Bright, followed by Dan Newcome and Lam Bowen, came up to join him, their faces filled with relief. Mayenne was falling back; the battle was all but over, and the sun was barely up.

'Why don't you sit?' Revill said. 'If I had a flagon of something, I'd get it out now… Corporal?' He eyed Tom Bright. 'Have you been hiding a jug I don't know about?'

'Not here, Captain,' the other replied. 'But I might find something later.' With that he slumped down beside Revill, and the other two followed. Lam Bowen, breathing fast, was grinning from ear to ear… but Dan Newcome shook his head.

'There's many a good man been slain down there, Captain,' he murmured. 'Yet many more have got clean away. The country will be full of fugitives…whether the King has them hunted down, or whether he doesn't, the League isn't finished.'

'That's true,' Revill said, after a moment. 'Mayenne may have lost a battle, but he will retire and regroup. There are too many who will never accept Henri as their King.'

They fell silent, their eyes returning to the battlefield, which was still a blur of movement. Some of the infantrymen had only now reached the heart of the struggle, to find that they were hardly needed. There were fewer horses visible now, as Mayenne's cavalry had retreated – to reveal the sobering sight of dead and injured, scattered about the churned-up field. Here and there, some of Henri's soldiers were despatching the enemy wounded: a pitiless thrusting of swords into thrashing bodies. They would spare most of the French, it emerged later, but the Spanish and others were shown no mercy. A sombre mood fell over the watching gun crews. La Guiche's men, though flushed with victory, stood in silence as they observed the carnage: the aftermath of the Battle of Ivry.

But on a sudden, there was another stir: shouts, and cheering.

'The King!' A voice nearby shouted. 'He does not stop!'

It was La Guiche. Getting to his feet, Revill started towards him. The French gunners began talking anxiously.

'I fear he is drunk with victory,' the artillery master said breathlessly. 'He crosses the Eure.' He pointed into the far distance, towards the river. Revill gazed, but could only make out a mass of horsemen, riding from the battlefield in a body. If the King was leading them, he was lost to sight.

'Pursuing stragglers,' he said. 'He knows their horses are tired – he's taking the chance to cut them down while he can.'

'But that is not a task for a King.' La Guiche was frowning. 'He could be cut off himself, even killed.'

'Somehow, I doubt it,' Revill said. 'It's his day, is it not?'

'Well, I suppose… a triumph, for the proud Bourbons.' The artillery master sighed. 'At times like these, Captain, I am glad I only have my guns to care for.' With that, he clapped Revill on the back and walked off to his men, who gathered about him.

And on a sudden, Revill's heart was heavy. It was over… he, Bright and the others could make preparations to go home. And yet a cloud hung over him, as the memory of his unpleasant encounter with the ensign came back. In the eyes of some, he was branded a coward. Could he simply leave… leave France, with that accusation hanging over him?

He could not, he decided. Though how he might remedy the matter, he did not know.

***

In the end, fears for the King's safety proved unfounded: he returned victorious from across the River Eure, and the rear guard instead was sent to pursue *liguer* fugitives. Eventually, news would come that the enemy had been chased all the way to the Seine – but for now, there was simply relief that the day had been won.

The English gunners returned to their tent, having accompanied Fiery Moll back with the packhorses. Now that victory had been assured and proclaimed, a mood of near-euphoria was spreading throughout the encampment. Tom Bright produced a flagon of cheap wine, and the crew drank to their success. They also drank the King's health, and finally Queen Elizabeth's. But by then, Revill had left them to celebrate and gone outside to gather his thoughts. He was still thinking, seated on a wooden box by the artillerymen's small cooking-fire, when a horseman appeared from somewhere, reined in and called his name. He stood up, seeing a young French soldier who looked vaguely familiar… and gave a start.

'You?' As the man dismounted, Revill stepped forward in disbelief. 'In God's name…'

He broke off. Standing before him was the same *brigadier* of horse who had brought him the challenge to a duel issued by Captain Dufort, back at Falaise. It seemed an age ago… and yet, with what had happened since, he felt his anger rise. Before the other could speak, he had put a hand to his sword-hilt.

'Captain, one moment.' The young man stepped back. 'Whatever you think, I assure you-'

'You'll assure me of nothing,' Revill said. 'In fact, it's I who should be issuing a summons to single combat – is that why you've come? Unfinished business, between your commander and myself? Well, I accept his challenge – with pleasure. Only, this time I'll not come alone - and the first thing we will require is an assurance that my opponent is not wearing armour-'

'There is no such summons! Please, I beg you to listen!'

Cut off in mid-flow, Revill took a closer look at the other's face: flushed, and streaked with dirt. And he noticed something else: blood stains on his coat, and a bandage about one hand. The young *brigadier* had been in the thick of battle… letting go of the sword-hilt, he exhaled.

'Forgive my rashness,' he murmured. 'In view of what I learned yesterday… the accusations I have heard levelled against me, I thought of one thing, and one thing only.'

'*Oui*… I understand.' Letting out a breath himself, the other managed a nod. 'And yet, I am not sent by the man you thought. Indeed…' he paused, then: 'I should tell you, *monsieur*, that Captain Dufort will not be in a position to issue challenges to anyone. He is among the fallen - one of the King's troops who will not rise again.'

A moment passed. Revill met his eye, a frown creasing his brow. 'You mean…?'

'I do. He was slain, cut through the neck… even his cuirass could not save him.'

They both fell silent. From the gunners' tent a roar of laughter erupted; Bright, Newcome and Bowen were celebrating still.

'Your pardon…' With a nod to the young man, Revill gestured him towards the fire. He accepted, but remained standing. When Revill offered him refreshment, he shook his head.

'I was sent to carry word to you, Captain,' he said. 'But of a very different nature to… to what occurred before, back in January. In short, you are summoned to attend the King.'

'I'm what?' Revill stared at him. 'Is this a mistake – or a jest?'

'It is neither, sir,' the other answered stiffly. 'I… well, in truth it's not my place to speak of this. But given your suspicions, I… I will say that before he died, Captain Dufort made confession to a priest. He expressed regret for his sins… and in the end he even spoke of what passed, on that day you and he met in the *bois* at Falaise. He gave account of his dishonourable actions, and asked that word be sent to the Marshal. Hence…'

'Good God!'

As the young man's words sank in, Revill almost staggered. A cloud was lifting… and now, he was eager to press the bringer of news to take a cup of wine and speak further. This was not the time – and yet, he wished to hear it spelled out.

'Can I assume that the accusations against me are proved invalid, then?' He asked. 'More, that Sir John Burgh has been informed? I tried to see him yesterday, only…'

'I'm certain that word will reach him, if it has not already,' came the reply, somewhat abruptly. 'But see now, I have given you a false impression. His Majesty wishes you to attend him, but not in relation to the matter of the duel. As you would guess, he has much to occupy him just now. The… business between you and Captain Dufort will soon be forgotten.'

'Yes… of course.' Feeling chastened, Revill looked away. Had he been so preoccupied with his reputation that he had lost sight of what surrounded him? With a glance towards the gunners' tent, from which sounds of merriment persisted, he faced the young man anew.

'Might I ask your name?' He enquired.

'It's Marais, monsieur.'

'Well, Marais… Revill attempted a smile. 'Firstly, I should thank you for your news… news that brings relief, despite the circumstances in which it was revealed. The death of any soldier in battle is a tragedy – and no shame should attach to Captain Dufort now. And of course, I will

204

be honoured to attend the King – am I to come at once? Moreover, can I ask what it is he requires of me?'

'Indeed, monsieur,' came the reply. 'If you will fetch your horse, we can go together. As for the service…' he frowned. 'You are wanted as a witness, to confirm what we already believe: that a certain commander of mercenaries is not whom he claims to be.'

Revill stared - and unbidden, an oath slipped from his mouth. 'This commander of mercenaries,' he said. 'Do you know his name?'

'He calls himself Brunner,' Marais replied. 'He leads a force of Swiss – or he does now, since their commander was slain. They have been surrounded, but are demanding surrender terms. Brunner claims to be a loyal follower of the Duc de Mayenne, who has served him throughout the campaign.'

He paused and put on a dour expression - but already, Revill knew what was coming.

'Yet, I know him by another name, monsieur,' Marais added. 'And so will you. Until two months ago he was fighting for the King, before he chose to turn. His name is Jannes Werner. Now, will you make ready to ride?'

Revill breathed in deeply, and nodded.

FOURTEEN

A short time later, Revill was admitted to King Henri's spacious campaign tent, having surrendered his weapons at the entrance. Sentries stood about, while officers who were gathered turned at his arrival. Some of them eyed him suspiciously as he walked towards the unmistakeable figure of the King himself, seated in a padded chair. Marais had accompanied him, but had now disappeared. There were others nearby... and at sight of one of them, he stiffened.

On his knees to one side, guarded by soldiers, was the man who had been present at the aborted duel at Falaise – and who had subsequently approached Revill and his crew with the offer to turn mercenary. Captain Werner – hatless, dishevelled, yet seemingly defiant to the last – looked up sharply, recognised him, and dropped his gaze at once.

Revill ignored him, and made his bow to the monarch.

It was his first sight at close quarters of Henri of Navarre: neat-bearded and elegant, still wearing armour with a red sash across his chest. He had removed his helmet with the distinctive plume, which now sat on a side-table. As Revill raised his head, the monarch at once began to address him in fluid, high-flown French. Mercifully, however, before he could make excuses for his failure to understand certain words, an interpreter hurried forward. In relief, Revill turned aside… and stiffened.

Arabella, in her role as Guy Baildon, met his eye briefly, then began to translate.

'His Royal Highness has heard report of you, Captain Revill,' she said. 'How you hurried to warn him of the approach of the Count of Egmont's force from Flanders. Even though the news was stale, he appreciates the effort.'

Revill inclined his head politely.

'Yet now,' she continued, 'he asks you to perform another small service for him. This man…' She turned to indicate Werner, who kept his eyes on the ground. 'This man, who commanded a force of Switzers serving the enemy, claims to be a Captain Brunner, with connections to important leaders in his country. He has demanded favourable terms of surrender for himself and his men. However, there are some who believe he is a traitor, who previously fought for the King's cause at Alençon and Falaise, before abandoning our army to serve the League. Such treachery demands retribution.'

She paused, leaving Revill impressed once again - not merely by her facility with the language, nor even with her ability to make everyone believe she was a man: it was the knowledge that she had somehow accounted for her recent absence, and got herself reinstated. Keeping expression from his face, he turned his gaze upon Werner… whereupon King Henri spoke up again, this time with a trace of anger.

'Listen carefully, Captain,' Arabella said, once the King had ceased. 'His Royal Highness has been informed that you were seen talking privately with this man, back at Falaise. He would be obliged, therefore, if you will tell the assembled company what you know, and confirm what others already suspect. Will you do so now?'

With that she fell silent and waited – and to Revill's embarrassment, all eyes were now on him, even the King's. But as he summoned the words one thought flew up, leaving him in little doubt: it was Arabella herself who, hearing rumours of his suspected cowardice, had wanted to set the record straight – and with the capture of Werner, whom she too would remember from the aborted duel, she had seen an opportunity and seized it.

'I will,' he said firmly. 'Here is my testimony: that the man you see here is Captain Jannes Werner, who was indeed part of the forces fighting for the King. But when Falaise was taken, and Lord Willoughby's troops about to depart for Caen, this man came to me and invited myself and my gunners to accompany him in going east, to join the Duc de Mayenne. His words, I remember well: he called this a dirty war between Frenchmen, and none of our concern. We should bring our guns, and fight for gain, he urged – for are English gunners not prized, throughout all of Europe?'

He paused to allow Arabella to translate, and at once a murmur went round the company. There were some dark looks thrown at Werner, who at last appeared agitated.

208

When it seemed as if he would protest, a soldier slapped a hand across his mouth to silence him.

Revill looked to the King, and put a hand on his heart. 'This I swear, on my honour,' he said.

'*Bon... c'est assez.*' Having expressed satisfaction, King Henri favoured him with a royal nod. With that he turned aside, beckoned one of his commanders forward and fell into conversation with him: so, the service had been performed, and Revill was dismissed. As he turned to go, he threw a last glance at Werner – who raised his eyes, and threw him a malevolent look: one devoid of human feeling. And if he had felt the slightest pang of regret for what he had done – helped send the man to certain death – it shrank to nothing.

Thereafter, somewhat abruptly, he found himself ushered out of the tent and into weak sunshine, where a boy was holding his horse. Having retrieved his sword and pistol he took the rein, but before he could mount there came a voice from behind, which he knew at once.

'You did right,' Arabella said.

'I might say the same for you,' Revill replied, turning to face her. Suddenly, he felt a smile forming; troubles of one sort or another seemed to have faded away, as the ringing in his ears had lifted. 'And I'm pleased to see you recovered from your... our adventure.'

But she did not return the smile. 'I've had time to think, since we parted,' she said, speaking low. 'I owe you much – and now, by a stroke of fortune, I've found a way to

209

repay you. Those wicked rumours that were spread, about you fleeing the field at Falaise because you were afraid of Captain Dufort... I was outraged. A part of me wished I'd never stopped the duel that day, but allowed you to fight and give Dufort the trouncing he deserved – which I know you would have done. As for those haughty commanders who were only too ready to believe the tale, so long as it was an Englishman who was accused...' she shook her head. 'Well, let me say that not all were of the same mind - Marshal Biron, for one. After hearing how Lord Willoughby had spoken for you, he agreed – and more, I'm sure Sir John Burgh never believed it either, in his heart. You should attend him soon, and assure yourself.'

'I believe I will,' Revill said. He might have added that when he did so, he would not allow a pompous ensign to stand in his way... but somehow, as things stood it didn't seem to matter. Eyeing Arabella, about to take what would surely be their last farewell, he paused. She wore a sober look - and on a sudden, a warning rang in his head.

'What is it?' He asked sharply... then when she hesitated, his face fell. Once again, to his dismay, the young messenger put a hand in her sleeve, and drew out a tightly-folded paper...

'Oh, by the Christ.'

Revill looked away, sagging as he spoke. About him, the massed tents, horse-lines, wagons and men - the entire encampment - seemed to become a blur. At last, after giving way to a series of soldierly oaths, he forced himself to face the one who – had he forgotten? – was in the end, a fellow-intelligencer who served the Queen's spymaster in London... and once again, gloom descended at sight of the paper, with its familiar seal.

'Well, what does he want of me this time?' he asked, without troubling to hide his anger. 'To play the turncoat, like our friend Werner - or just to murder someone? For I'm the willing pair of hands, am I not? A mastiff on a chain, there to savage whomever his master wishes – and you're just the messenger again, are you not? Another pair of hands...'

But he broke off. He might have spoken further, even called back some of his words, but Arabella stayed him. Laying a hand on his sleeve, she forced him to meet her eye.

'If I could throw this paper on the nearest fire, I would do it,' she said. 'With all my heart, I despise how Heneage uses you. But you know I cannot... how I've no choice but to obey orders. Remember, I beg, what I told you – what no-one else knows, save Heneage himself. You are the only friend I have here... perhaps the only friend I have in all of Christendom. And I would not have you despise me – more than anything, I would hate that.'

They were silent, standing close together; almost as close as when they'd shared a bed in a ruined hut on the road to Dreux. Her courage, even more than her loyalty, humbled him again; with a sigh, he took the paper from her hand and stowed it inside his coat.

'I could never despise you,' he said. 'And wherever you are, know that I'm still your friend – one who would come to your aid at any time.' Taking the reins of his horse, he put out his other hand. At once she squeezed it, then stepped back with a look of relief.

'I haven't read it,' she said, meaning the paper. 'Not this time. But if it contains the kind of orders you fear it might, I have a suggestion: burn it, and send word to me.' She summoned a smile. 'For in truth, it's a miracle that any despatch should reach me here, is it not? Messages go astray often – especially in war. If I receive word from you, I will deny all knowledge of having seen this letter. Let Heneage berate me all he likes.'

'He would be a fool to do so,' Revill said, returning her gaze. 'As I will tell him when I reach London, whenever that may be. But just now, I've a gun crew some way off, who are most likely drunk. I'd best go and see they don't get into a fight with the French.'

And with that he turned, put foot in stirrup and hauled himself into the saddle. Then he was riding away, without looking back.

Guy Baildon, despatch-rider, watched him until he disappeared from sight.

***

A short time later Revill was sat by the cooking-fire at the gunners' camp. There was no wine left to drink, but he had accepted a mug of cider from the French gunners. They had gone off with La Guiche, to dismantle their

212

battery. Most of the King's troops would be leaving soon; once again, the talk was of Henri's impatience to reach Paris and lay siege to it again, where he had failed before. The war, of course, would roll on.

Revill had wished the artillery master well, promising to take farewell later. His own crew, meanwhile, he had left dozing in the tent. It was not merely the wine; he knew they were exhausted, as was every man who had done his part that day. And yet there was activity about the encampment: wounded men being cared for, and dead ones being buried. Time enough to pack up when we're rested, he reasoned. In fact, the only cloud on the horizon was the folded paper inside his coat: the order from Heneage that as yet, he had not read.

Now, alone as he was, he could delay it no longer. With a sigh he took it out, broke the seal and spread it out, blinked, and read it twice over. Then, despite its grim contents, he threw back his head and laughed... the first real laugh he could remember in weeks.

Still laughing, he balled the paper up in his fist and was about to throw it into the fire, when there came a sound close by. Turning, he saw Lam Bowen appear from the tent looking somewhat sheepish.

'Captain?' The young gunner walked over, coughed and wiped his mouth with the back of his hand. 'Your pardon... the corporal said I should get the fire started, heat up some broth.'

'I lit it myself, as you can see,' Revill told him, his laughter subsiding. 'But no matter. You'd best heat the broth anyway, for the hungry men here…' Then as a thought occurred, he frowned. 'As it happens, I've an errand for you first. Will you run that for me, quick as you can?' And when the boy nodded: 'There's something I want you to take to the King's quarters. Ask for an English messenger named Baildon – Guy Baildon – and give him this.'

Whereupon he placed the balled paper on the fire, waited until it curled and started to burn, then snatched it from the flames. Watched by a mystified Lam Bowen, Revill then tore a piece from one corner, keeping its charred edge, and threw the rest of it back to be consumed. Holding up the fragment, he waited for the boy to take it.

'Is that all there is, Captain?' Lam asked.

'That's all,' Revill replied. 'Give it to Master Baildon, and no-one else – let no-one else even see it. If he's absent, wait for his return… we'll save some broth for you. There's no other message,' he added. 'He will understand.' With that, he waited until Bowen had trotted off before turning back to the fire.

With satisfaction, he watched Sir Thomas Heneage's last instruction to him in France burn to ashes. And for some time after he remained seated, brooding on events, before allowing himself to dwell again on the contents of the paper: a few terse, business-like paragraphs in the man's distinctive hand. Finally he frowned, shaking his head at the brutality of it – not to mention the absurdity.

In clear and precise terms, he had been ordered to take the life of the despatch-rider with whom he had worked, on the mission to the English ambassador in Paris. Once that task was completed, and with Heneage's second instruction too – to wit, the removal of the agent John Garratt – Revill was to find a means to isolate the one known as Guy Baildon, kill him and dispose of the body. Should the opportunity arise whereby the corpse could be concealed among others – enemy combatants, for example - that was all to the good.

Baildon, Heneage was suggesting, was no longer to be trusted. Revill shook his head and, once again, cursed the spymaster and his over-wrought suspicions roundly. One day, he half-suspected - perhaps when he too was believed to have outlived his purpose – an order would go out for Revill himself to be eliminated: *snuffed out*, in Heneage's phrase. In the meantime, he refused to kill anyone – especially someone like Arabella: his friend unto death.

He was still seated by the fire a half hour later when Lam Bowen returned, out of breath and sweating. After waiting some time to see Guy Baildon, the boy had run the whole distance from the King's camp. Coming to a halt, he almost fell to his knees.

'Cheer yourself, Lam,' Revill said. 'If you'll fetch Corporal Bright, I'll send him over to bargain with one of the French sutlers. We'll not have broth, but beef or pork

– and a pudding, the best they'll sell us. And wine too… does that please you?' But when the boy nodded and broke into a smile, his captain drew him closer.

'Was all well, when you delivered my token? Did he say anything?'

'He said not a word, Captain,' Lam replied. 'But he gave me ten sols.' Having said that he would have moved away - but Revill saw the look on his face, and called him back.

'There's more, isn't there?' Forcing the boy to meet his eye, he put on a stern look. 'Come now – don't dissemble. Tell me all.'

The boy gulped, and reddened as he stood. 'Your pardon, sir,' he stammered. 'For it… well, in truth I'm ashamed to speak of it, but if you will have it so-'

'I will,' Revill said. 'Speak, and be done with it.'

'He… Baildon… he kissed me, sir – on the lips!' The boy blurted. 'Now I pray you, don't say a word about it to the other men, will you? For I'll never hear the last till the day I die!'

For a while Revill said nothing… then, having teased the boy long enough, he broke into a smile. 'Your secret is safe,' he said. 'Now, will you go and rouse the corporal?'

At which the boy's relief was so great, he had to hide another smile as he hurried off.

Then at last, with everything said and sifted, he allowed himself to think of the return journey to England… and to London…

And finally, to Jenna.

216

FIFTEEN

When the over-crowded French merchantman dropped anchor at the port of Dover, on a blustery morning in early April, Revill and his gunners were among the first to take a boat ashore and set foot on the quay. There they stood in a tight group, breathed English air for the first time in many months, and looked about for the nearest inn. Naturally there was one close by, generally frequented by sailors.

'I'll take a mug,' Revill said, 'then I must leave you and hire a horse - it's more than a sixty-mile ride to London.' He eyed each man in turn, with warm respect. Now, at the end of it all, ragged and weary yet in good spirits, they were loth to part.

'Me, I'll be finding a bed here for the night, Captain,' Tom Bright said. 'I don't plan on going home until tomorrow.'

'That's well,' Revill nodded. 'And I'll pay... for all of you,' he added. 'Enjoy the day, sleep like dogs tonight in Dover, and God speed thereafter.'

He did not add that this was the last time he expected to see Dan Newcome and Lam Bowen. His soldiering days, he had resolved, were over. On reaching London, he had to see Jenna. But first he intended to face Sir Thomas

Heneage… the thought made his mouth tighten. With a glance round the bustling harbour front, he led the way to the tavern.

At this hour the place was quiet. Revill took a table by the window, then called for ale and tobacco. Within minutes the four of them were clinking mugs, Revill and Newcome puffing on well-filled pipes. But as they settled and began to talk, his gaze wandered to the window, from there to the grey sea beyond where ships rode at anchor – and soon, his thoughts drifted.

His farewells, back at the encampment on the plain beside Ivry, had been brief. He and La Guiche had shared a cup of wine, standing in a breeze before his tent. They then parted with a promise to dine together again, should Revill ever return to service in France. And though that, he felt certain, would never happen, he had not the heart to voice it. His last sight of the man, moustache twitching impressively, was of him striding off to give orders. The King's army was moving eastward, doubtless to another battle; his hope was that the good-hearted artillery master would come through it.

He had gone off then, to make preparations for Fiery Moll's journey to the coast. Before leaving, however, he had a brief audience with Sir John Burgh, which he had dreaded. And yet, to his relief, the meeting was warm. The commander had now been better informed of Revill's activities, and was eager to dismiss the accusations some had levelled against him. He had received a most

218

favourable report from Marshal Biron, he said, which spoke of Revill's steadfastness and courage. As for his decision to leave the King's service and return to England: Sir John was sorry to lose a good officer. After all, he had added, English gunners were prized throughout Europe – even by the Great Turk himself. Did Revill know that?

Revill did know it, and expressed pride in his own crew. He was also tempted to enquire about the favourable report from Marshal Biron, whom he had never met: he had a strong idea as to the true source of such praise. But he dismissed it, bade Burgh a formal good-bye, and left him with a lighter heart.

Outside the tent, he paused to eye the same stuffy, heavy-browed ensign who had previously denied him access to the commander. At sight of him the man flinched - and though words sprang to Revill's lips, chiefly in regard to a shabby accusation of cowardice, he chose a mild approach.

'Did you hear that Captain Dufort was killed in battle?' He asked, in a casual tone. And when the other made no answer: 'Such a pity - for a keen duellist, I mean. Even his cuirass couldn't save him.' At which the ensign had swallowed, until with a final glance Revill had left him...

'Your pipe, Captain!'

With a jolt, he was plunged back into the present. He looked round to see Tom Bright pointing, and blinked: smouldering shreds of tobacco had fallen from his pipe, which he had lowered unthinkingly, and fallen into his mug. At sight of his pained expression, the three gunners guffawed.

'To the devil with my carelessness.' Their captain put a finger into his ale, trying to catch up the offending fragments, then gave up. With a sigh he raised the mug, put it to his lips and drained it to the last. The result was a cheer from his crew, and some renewed clinking. And a half hour later, when Revill had handed over money for their food and board, they shook hands and made ready to part. All three of them stood to drink his health, before lowering their eyes in sudden embarrassment.

'Remember what I told you once, Newcome?' Revill said. 'You're too old for soldiering. While you, Bowen...' He turned to the youngest. 'You're too young. Back to London with you – and I wish you a merry life.'

With that, he turned swiftly and headed for the door. Tom Bright accompanied him outside, the two of them standing in the windy street.

'The Three Cranes in the Vintry, Captain,' the corporal said, somewhat too breezily. 'You said we'd get falling-down drunk, remember - and you would pay. I mean to hold you to it!'

'I'll not disappoint,' Revill said with a smile. 'Now back in the tavern with you – and don't get into a tussle.'

Whereupon they embraced swiftly and tightly, then drew apart just as quickly. Bright turned without a word, shoved the inn door open and let it bang shut behind him.

***

The following morning, after a gruelling ride to London which had taken up the remainder of the previous day, Revill waited for the Great South Gate to open before leading his hired horse under the archway and across the already-bustling London Bridge. Having spent the night at a low inn in Southwark and left without a breakfast, he was tired, hungry and dirty. He was also stiff in several places, and the wound in his side had begun to trouble him again. Yet his mind was set, his purpose undimmed: to stand before Sir Thomas Heneage and face the worst. He had done all he could, he would say: obeyed every order, and returned ready to answer any charge the Vice-Chamberlain might throw at him. Looking grimly ahead, he emerged on Fish Street, remounted and rode to the corner with East Cheap.

At the crossing, he paused. He had been thinking to make his way to Sir Francis Walsingham's house in Seething Lane, where he had last met with Heneage. But now he remembered: the man had a chamber at Whitehall, and with Sir Francis's worsening health, had spoken of moving there. So, with the hubbub of London all about him, Revill made his laborious way through the entire length of the city, finally emerging at Ludgate. From there he rode to Westminster and then through the gates of Whitehall Palace, where he dismounted. A short time later, having given account of himself to the guards as an officer returning from France, he was walking along a passage as directed – only to be told that he was too early.

Sir Thomas was not yet come to the palace, a secretary said… and more, there were others who would be seeking an audience. Would the captain care to depart, then return later in the day? Or did he wish to present a petition?

The captain would not depart - nor did he have a petition, Revill replied. Whereupon he found a bench in an ante-room, put down his stained soldier's coat, and made himself as comfortable as he could. Unsurprisingly, he was asleep within minutes. The next thing he knew, someone was shaking him by the shoulder and mumbling in his ear. Waking with a start, he looked up into the unsmiling face of the secretary.

'Captain Revill?' The man murmured. 'You are fortunate… Sir Thomas can give you a moment, before he is needed in Council.'

'How long have I been here?' He asked, suppressing a yawn. But without replying, the other moved off to a door and opened it. Drawing a breath and shaking himself mentally, he got up and walked through into the room beyond. At once, the door closed behind him.

'By God, Revill… you are a most wretched sight.'

He froze, finding himself in a small chamber with a tiny window. Candles illuminated the gloom… while before him, behind a table stacked with papers, sat the Vice-Chamberlain himself. The two of them locked eyes, before Revill forced himself to make his bow.

'Your pardon for my appearance, sir,' he said in a toneless voice. 'I've been somewhat occupied with the war... you'll have heard about it, I'm sure.'

'Most amusing,' Heneage replied drily. 'Now, I did harbour a hope that you'd have sent me a report, but once again I was disappointed. Do you have anything to tell me?'

Revill found his anger rising, but controlled it. Heneage, unchanged apart from a suit of fine clothes he had not seen before, wore his sardonic look. A small bell sat on his table, by means of which he could summon his secretary in a moment. Sitting back in his chair, the spymaster waited.

'I killed John Garratt, if that's what's troubling you,' Revill said finally.

'I know that. Baildon's report reached me some time ago...' The Vice-Chamberlain paused, raising an eyebrow. 'Don't you have news of him?'

'He was in good health when I last saw him – sir. That was following the battle at Ivry. He performed well, as did all the English. I cannot speak highly enough of all of them, in particular my gunners...'

He broke off, for Heneage was frowning.

'The prowess of your gunners is not my concern, Revill,' he said impatiently. 'You had orders of a different nature – or had you forgotten?'

'I don't forget anything,' Revill replied quietly. On a sudden, the matter of his servitude to this man had risen with a vengeance: the chain by which he was bound, on account of his sister and her conversion to Popery. Over the past weeks, with all that had happened in France, he had almost dared to hope that the Vice-Chamberlain might release him from such constraint... but seeing the man's cold stare, his heart sank.

'With your leave, sir,' he added, 'I have a wound that needs attention. I'm weary, and eager to take rest among people who know me. Is there anything more you require, before I may be released?'

'Released?' Heneage echoed, savouring the word. 'Well now, that would depend...' he assumed a weak smile. 'In truth, I've yet to decide whether your service has been adequate. Ever since you departed last year, I seem to have been forced to rely on others for intelligence – though you were told that I expected reports. Now, I find myself in the dark still, regarding the person I just spoke of. Do you tell me you received no order regarding Baildon?'

'I do,' Revill said, without expression.

'Well, I find that difficult to believe,' came the reply. 'Our messengers have always given prompt and efficient service – even when obliged to cross the Channel and ride across vast swathes of France.' He paused, then: 'Sir Francis's reach has always been long, Revill – from Scotland in the north, to Spain and even as far as Constantinople. I have sought to preserve that reach – perhaps even to extend it. Am I making myself clear?'

With that, the man fell silent. But since it was clear to Revill that he was not to be allowed to leave just yet, he took a breath and spoke up.

'In regard to the one I know as Guy Baildon, I have nothing further to tell,' he said. 'We carried out your orders in Paris, then made our way to the King's camp on the Plain of Saint André. Following the battle, we parted - and that is all.'

Taut as a wand, and feeling dispirited on a sudden, he stood his ground. His mind had flown back to his last meeting with Arabella... he felt her hand on his sleeve, saw her anxious face, and lowered his gaze. Just then, he felt inclined to turn his back on the Vice-Chamberlain and walk from the room. With a heavy heart he waited, whereupon...

'Very well.'

He looked up sharply, and was surprised to see Heneage pass a hand wearily across his face. Was it his imagination, or did the man look strained – even twitchy? Given the number of brutal executions he had ordered, Revill wondered, was there some part of him, after all, that balked at it? Might he even – perish the thought - have a heart?

For a moment, the Vice-Chamberlain looked down at the papers on his desk, his lips pressed tightly together. Then he looked up, met Revill's gaze and gave a curt nod.

'You may leave,' he said, in a flat tone. 'Go to your red-haired Cornishwoman, rest, and seek a surgeon for your wound. I have no further business with you… for the present.' Then, having allowed the last words to sink in, he added: 'But be under no illusion, Revill: our agreement stands, and I will call on you again. Now take yourself away - and buy a new set of clothes. I'll even reimburse you.'

With that, he turned to a small chest on his table – the same one Revill recalled in Walsingham's house, from what seemed a long time ago. With a flourish the man opened it, drew out a small purse and threw it – rather too hard. This time Revill failed to catch it; it landed by his feet, obliging him to stoop and pick it up.

His pride, he would think later, might have made him leave it on the floor and walk out; but just then, pride was among the least of his concerns. Without another word, but without making a bow, he turned about and headed for the door. As he went, he allowed himself one last glance back at the man who, despite everything, still ruled him, and saw him bend quickly to his papers.

***

Less than a half hour later, with rain clouds threatening overhead, he arrived at the house of the haberdasher Jonas Stephens in Lombard Street, where he dismounted. He let the horse's reins trail, narrowly avoided a puddle and walked to the doorway. The door was open, and there were customers, and a murmur of voices… a day of business like any other. The war in France, so vivid in his mind, might have been taking place in the Indies for all these people knew or cared. Tiredly, he tramped forward in his heavy boots... and saw her.

She was talking with a gentlewoman in a fine embroidered gown; talking of taffeta and silk, and blackwork. But as Revill drew near, his sword clinking at his side, her gaze flew up, causing her to falter. Finally, murmuring some excuse to the customer, she moved unhurriedly from the rear of the shop, to stand before him. Without a word, he drew her outside into the street.

'Promise me one thing – before anything else,' she breathed. 'That you will never go to war again. Swear it on your honour - now.'

Revill met her gaze, put a hand on his sword and smiled, even as he swore.

Now at last he could rest... for a while, at least.

Printed in Great Britain
by Amazon

18346361R00133